Wild Cotton

Helen Pereira

Also by Helen Pereira:
MAGPIE IN THE TOWER
Creative Publishers – 1990

THE HOME WE LEAVE BEHIND
Killick Press – 1992

Wild Cotton

Helen Pereira

Killick Press
an imprint of Creative Publishers
St. John's, Newfoundland
1994

©1994 —Helen Pereira

Appreciation is expressed to *The Canada Council* for publication assistance.

Cover from a photograph by Michael J. Thomas

Printed in Canada by
ROBINSON-BLACKMORE PRINTING & PUBLISHING LTD.
P.O. Box 8660, St. John's, Newfoundland A1B 3T7

Published by
KILLICK PRESS (AN IMPRINT OF CREATIVE PUBLISHERS)
A Division of Robinson-Blackmore Printing & Publishing Ltd.
P.O. Box 8660, St. John's, Newfoundland A1B 3T7

Canadian Cataloguing in Publication Data

Pereira, Helen, 1926–

    Wild cotton
    ISBN 1-895387-31-0

I. Title

PS8581.E648W45 1994   C813'.54   C94-950006-2
PR9199.3.P57W45 1994

For Michael

Contents

Foreign Correspondent

1

Bell Curves

49

Green and Gold

67

Wild Cotton

85

Tape Recorder

111

The Coronation

123

Futures

131

Acknowledgements

The author wishes to express her gratitude to her Cleveland workshop colleagues, Ethna Carroll, Daniel Chaon, Jeff Erdrie, Sheryl Hawkins, and Hugh Kennedy; to her Cuban connection, Lisa Makarchuk; to word processors Teresa Walsh and David Kines; and to her editors Faye Ode and Don Morgan.

Some of these stories appeared in different versions in *Antigonish Review, Canadian Woman's Studies, Whiskey Island (U.S.A.),* and *The Great Canadian Murder and Mystery Stories* (Quarry Press).

foreign correspondent

September, 1962

I SHOULD have worn the pink silk dress with the low back, Amy thinks, as she passes the rows of Africans in brightly-coloured batiks; the row of Indians in Nehru jackets with their sari-clad wives. She tries to identify the flags of various nations flying at each aisle, to translate the signs in Spanish, naming occupants of the reserved front rows. She had thought her olive green shirtmaker dress would make her look more business-like, more like a journalist, but now she realizes it's exactly the same colour as the Cuban militia uniforms, which seem to be everywhere, so she feels nondescript and tired in her stale, sticky dress in spite of this momentous occasion.

A smiling teen-aged student in white blouse and navy skirt proudly ushers Amy down to the vacant front rows. The girl's outfit worries Amy, because she sees it everywhere on young women. It seems to be the uniform of students, and Amy equates uniformity with totalitarianism. She decides that the North American press must be right about Cuba. The girl beams proudly as she stops at an aisle and directs Amy into the empty row marked by the Canadian flag and a painted sign—*El Cuerpo Diplomatico do Canada*. At first Amy feels a thrill of excitement at her luck in achieving this prestigious front row seating, but when she realizes there will probably be no real Canadian diplomats showing up, she looks around nervously, as if fearing that a Mountie will

1

appear and pronounce her an imposter. Right now, a Mountie would be a relief, a protection, because exhaustion and
heat have heightened Amy's imagination, her paranoia. Fantasies and reality merge, indistinct.

She has not slept since last night in Toronto. Early that
same morning she had boarded a Miami-bound Trans-
Canada Airlines plane. It was her very first flight, her very
first trip to a foreign country, her very first venture into
journalism. She hoped that now that her kids were older she
might become a foreign correspondent, begin a glamorous
new life as a celebrity and be invited to participate on TV
panel discussions. The expert on Cuba.

In the past she always remained behind at home with her
two children, seeing her husband Walter off at the airport.
Always with envy and yearning. Walter is an important
government official and has flown all over North America to
participate in seminars. An agronomist, he was even sent to
Africa by UNESCO. Once, back in Sioux Lookout when she
and the kids had seen him off for somewhere he had kissed
her goodbye and said, 'Never mind sweetie-pie. Maybe some
day, you will get to fly somewhere.' With a pang she used to
watch his plane disappear, feel her two pre-schoolers tug at
her arms, whimpering, 'Daddy.' She held Sandy the baby
with her left arm while trying to comfort her weeping three-
year-old daughter tugging at her right. Driving home she
wondered if it would be the same for her as always. Reading
the kids extra Dr. Seuss stories after their baths until they
slept to help ease their longing for the exciting important
Daddy. Then lying awake herself. Sometimes she read half
the night to fill her own emptiness.

Now it has finally happened. It is her turn. She is seated
in the Chaplin Theatre in Havana, waiting to hear a speech by
Fidel Castro. A shiver of excitement and fear runs through
her.

SHE cannot believe her day as she tries to remember it, tries to put the pieces together. Events are fragmented like a movie. A thriller. When had the movie—the drama—begun?

With those two Cubans at the Miami airport, who approached her and begged her to take serum to a sick child in Havana? Yes, with them. They had even addressed her by name, which amazed her.

'Señora Campbell? You are Señora Campbell from Toronto?' A short dark man asked while his taller companion watched. She swept back a long sheaf of hair that had fallen forward across her cheek, aware that the gesture was attractive, and pleased that the summer sun had left her very blonde. Her neighbour, Elsie, had told her Cubans went nuts over blondes.

'Yes. I am Señora Campbell.' She enjoyed identifying herself as *señora*, liked the sound of it, the feeling of being exotic and worldly.

'Please *señora*, take this medicine to my poor wife! My little girl is dying of polio. This is the serum.' The man handed her a small bottle. Amy hesitated at first because she had just finished reading a pamphlet about health reform in Cuba, which claimed that country to be the first in the world to have vaccinated all its citizens against polio with the new Sabin-Salk. Remembering this information, she was puzzled: she frowned. The man grasped her shoulder and his voice grew positively operatic with anguish. Amy pulled away and stared at his plump hand thrusting out the little bottle.

'I thought'...she began, then saw the distress, the pain on the man's face. She was too hot and tired to argue. And because he had left Cuba, he must not be aware of the revolution and would only deny what she had read about all their wonderful new health reforms. The two men waited, expectant, stood close in front of her, raving on to each other in Spanish. She caught *doente, muerte*. She sensed she was

being conned, as she often was by walk-ins on Friday after-
noons in the social agency where she worked. Inevitably she
could never get through by telephone to the busy welfare
offices to verify 'emergencies.' And, inevitably, she did what
her supervisor and conscience told her to do. When in doubt,
believe people. It was better to be conned than to let a family
suffer. Inevitably she forked over ten dollars of her own
because by Friday the agency was always out of petty cash.
This situation with the two Cubans was the same kind of
predicament. What if all that stuff about vaccination in the
pamphlet were propaganda? She sighed, aware that the men
were watching, waiting. Then she frowned, reached out and
took the bottle.

'All right. I'll bring it. But how—' Before she could continue, the dark man thrust the bottle into her hand, answered
her unfinished question.

'See this name and phone number here?' He pointed to a
label on the bottle. 'It is my wife. Phone her. She will come to
pick it up. I will phone her, also. Please, *señora*, where are you
staying?'

'*Havana Libre.*' She tossed off the hotel name nonchalant-
ly, feeling important. Nothing had actually been confirmed,
of course, but that was where she intended to stay. That was
how she'd answered the same question earlier in Toronto at
U.S. immigration.

'*Gracias, gracias, señora,*' the operatic man said. 'You will
save my daughter! God will bless you!' Before she could ask
further questions or reconsider, the two turned and darted
away, disappearing in the crowd.

Amy had looked at the bottle in her hand and felt annoyed and embarrassed. Annoyed because she feared she
might have been conned; embarrassed because the bottle
looked like a urine specimen. She slipped it into her purse,
deciding it to be a safer hiding-place than her shoulder bag.

She had already checked a huge suitcase containing enough clothes and books to last her six weeks—the length of time she decided it would take her to get to the bottom of all the political stuff about Russians and missile bases. Dramatic, sensational headlines in *The Toronto Telegram*. 10,000 RUSSIAN TROOPS LAND IN CUBA. U.S. FEARS INVASION.

Her husband Walter, a closet-Marxist, told her it was propaganda but that he wished it were true. She had dropped out of all the various groups they had joined because the rhetoric and endless meetings bored her. But Walter hung on and was on the executive of some of these organizations. He even corresponded with Cheddi Jagan, President of British Guyana.

She had originally planned to visit St. Pierre and Miquelon for her first flight—to brush up on her French—and perhaps to become a travel writer like her friend Libby. Libby had published a couple of travel pieces after a vacation in Ireland and subsequently landed a full-time job at *The Globe and Mail*. Libby's job involved a salary and paid travel expenses. Amy secretly held similar ambitions, but when she telephoned a travel agency to inquire about the French islands, she learned that she would have to change planes three times, take a ferry boat, and pay out over $700 for her ticket. More than she had budgeted. After this let-down, she set off for work, her dreams shot. On her way to the bus-stop she bemoaned her situation to Paddy Flynn, who worked for UPI. They usually caught the same bus. He had even encouraged her to write after she showed him a couple of her humorous essays. 'Go to Cuba, Amy. It's hot news now. No one is going there. The bureaus have pulled all their people out. I promise that I'll edit and help you place anything you write.' That did it.

Walter was elated. 'Good for you, Amy! I'm glad you're finally going to do something worthwhile, something political. I'll even give you one of my letters from Cheddi. He's been to Havana and is friendly with Fidel. His name might open some doors for you.'

'No thanks. I want to be objective. Handle what I see in my own way.'

Walter looked disappointed, fumbled with the letter, then managed a smile. 'Be that way then. I suppose I should allow that. It is your trip. You saved for it... I've never even been there. Wouldn't dare. Not with my job. Which reminds me. I doubt you'll publish anything, but if you do, use your own name. It might get me in hot water if people at work know you're my wife.'

'I'd intended to use my own name. It was good enough when I edited *The Ubyssey*.' She was rubbing it in, which she seldom did, that at university she had been the star, the-woman-into-everything on the campus, while Walter was a slumper who lurked in the library.

Walter walked away, fiddling with Cheddi's letter, and she felt sorry for him.

Next day she made an appointment with the Cuban consul who gave her the necessary information about documents and exit permits, a tiny cup of strong black coffee and a load of pamphlets before rhapsodizing about her hair. She escaped with a hug and a severe case of the giggles.

'I'm proud of you, Amy,' Walter told her three weeks later at the airport. She was scared and excited, worried about her children left sleeping in their beds. 'I'll be okay with the kids. It's your turn for adventure. You've waited a long time. I've lots of holidays left—I'll plan some education-al field trips with the kids. This will be a good experience for all of us.'

Amy fought the need to cling to Walter as he hugged her goodbye; felt a wrench of pain to be leaving her kids. Especially Emma, who cried. Even though the children were aged nine and twelve, it was her first separation from them.

But it was her turn. Finally. She always had resented seeing Walter off. Now she'd show him. Her anticipation became a frenzy as she worked hard late at night in order to leave the house in a manageable condition, and her clients' records up to date for her relief worker. She kept going over her worries in bed, occasionally nudging Walter, reminding him: 'Don't forget Sandy's dental appointment on September 12th,' or 'the kids' winter clothes have to be picked up at the dry-cleaners. And leave Emma's rock collection alone. She gets upset if it's rearranged.'

Walter was funny, she thought. Off to the Ontario Department of Agriculture clad in suit, briefcase in hand, to meet with bureaucrats. At home—when he was home—he affected T-shirts with revolutionary slogans, worn-out jeans and running shoes. The only thing red about him really was his hair, and his face, which when angry turned pink with ideological passion. And he was plump. Amy thought it would look better, even for a closet-Marxist, to be thin. And although he insisted that she work—Russian women did— he would not allow her to have a cleaning woman. 'That's elitist,' he said. So she had the housework as well.

By the time she was on the plane, Cuba-bound after a Miami stop, it was all history. She was preoccupied with her important task. Who to interview? Where to focus? Education, she thought, in this year of alphabetization. Or health?

She had encountered suspicion, even hostility, from U.S. immigration officials in Miami. 'You a diplomat?' an officer asked.

'No.'

'Then why on earth are you going to Havana? Everybody else is trying to get out.'

'I'm a journalist. That is, I want to be. I want to write about it. What's happening, down there.'

'It says there on your passport, occupation, social worker. Nothing about writing. Got a press card?'

'No. But I've a friend at UPI, he said he could help—'

'Where are you staying? What hotel?'

'*Havana Libre.*'

'You're asking for trouble.' The officer was short, fair, freckled. He frowned and strode away from her: showed her passport to another officer behind a counter in a glassed-in cubicle. This other officer rose, stared at her, shrugged, stamped the passport, handed it to the fair man who strode back and returned it to her with a disapproving look. Pointing, he said, 'Wait out there by Gate 3C.'

She felt guilty, as though she were breaking the law, smuggling, or spying for the enemy. At this point, she wasn't quite sure who the enemy was.

I'm overtired and hungry, she decided. I'll feel better after I've eaten. She headed to a lunch counter, sat down and ordered coffee and a toasted bacon sandwich. She wolfed it down, gulped her coffee, and felt better. For a short while. After she finished, she handed the cashier her counter check and a ten dollar bill.

'What the hell's that?' the cashier demanded, slapping the bill back to her.

'Ten dollars. Canadian.'

'It's no good here,' the cashier retorted. Amy heard stools swivel as people turned around to see what a Canadian looked like. She felt as though she'd been caught using counterfeit or Monopoly money. Redfaced, she reluctantly took out a traveller's cheque from her purse. She hadn't wanted to change any until she got to Havana. Fortunately the cheques were in U.S. dollars, but unfortunately were Thomas Cook, not American Express. The cashier took a long time examining it, frowning, then commanded, 'Sign.' Amy signed the cheque and waited while the cashier counted out U.S. bills, then picked up the bills and quickly shoved them into her purse.

She walked out of the coffee shop and looked up at signs, searching for Gate 3C. When she finally spotted it, in front sat a middle-aged couple on a bench. Good, she thought, I'll have company. I just need someone to talk to. I'm feeling defensive because of how I've been treated here. I don't feel guilty about the medicine. I should have stood up to the immigration officers, and to the cashier acting so bloody superior. Once upon a time U.S. money was less than ours. But we used to accept it at par, just to be nice.

She was comforted by the sight of the waiting couple. As she neared the bench she saw them more clearly. They seemed homey-looking and friendly. The plump, auburn-haired woman wore a powder-blue print dress with a low scooped neckline that showed freckled white skin. The man was redfaced, perhaps because he was wearing a tightly-knotted floral tie. His neck bulged over his shirt collar. Amy glanced at their luggage tags. Same code as hers. She sat down opposite them, removed her shoulder bag, and set it on the bench beside her.

'Are you going to Havana?' she asked.

'Yes.'

'Oh, I'm so glad! I was afraid I'd be the only one, that I'd be travelling all alone.'

They looked at her suspiciously—her new olive green dress, her stockings and heels, and especially at the white gloves she still wore in summer, even though people in Toronto teased her about it. Her mother had taught her that gloves were correct, so the habit stuck.

She wondered about this couple. They did not look like journalists. 'So what brings you two to Havana?' she asked. 'Will you be staying very long?'

'It's a missionary posting. We're evangelists,' the woman announced.

Amy had intended to identify herself as a journalist, once out of Canada, but figured that 'social worker' would go over better with missionaries.

'I'm a social worker,' she said. 'I'm curious about what they are doing down there. Social reform, health. The Cubans.'

The couple exchanged glances, picked up their *Good News Bibles* and began to read, cutting her off.

Well, I'll show them, she thought. I'll make it sound like my own mission. 'I'm bringing a special serum to Havana. There's this little girl...'

'You fell for that?' the woman asked. The couple slapped their books down, looked at her briefly and chuckled, nudging each other.

'They tried that on us, too,' the woman continued, 'but we'd been warned.' Suddenly serious, she said, 'You better be careful. It could be drugs, anything. You're taking a big chance.' Then she pointedly returned to her reading.

Increasingly edgy from sleeplessness, and now scared about the serum, Amy remembered all the awful stuff about Cuba she'd read in *The Telegram*. She could be imprisoned: she could disappear. She would never see Walter or her children again. And so far she'd been snubbed by everyone, even the missionaries. Except for the two Cubans. She reached for her bag and took out Alejo Carpentier's *The Lost Steps*. A magical novel which she loved. She found it hard to imagine the novelist as Cuba's Minister of Culture, as a bureaucrat. But then it was hard for her to imagine Castro—a Jesuit-educated lawyer—as a dictator.

She flipped through pages, not really reading, the way she used to back at university cramming for exams.

After an announcement on the intercom the couple rose and picked up their books and luggage. Amy did the same and saw a uniformed official slide open the gate. She followed the couple to the aircraft—a rickety turbo-prop. Just as she was about to ascend the steps a man rushed through the gate toward her and grabbed her shoulder. A very anxious man who said, 'The medicine! Did you get the medicine?'

'Yes,' she said, turning to smile before continuing up the steps.

'Thank God! My poor father! He needs this heart medicine to save his life.' Amy halted just inside the entrance after the impatient steward slid the door shut.

Polio serum. Heart medicine. Two different stories. She was relieved that the missionaries were well ahead, seated up front out of earshot.

What was she carrying? If it were drugs, she'd better think of something. But what if those men were counter-revolutionaries, or worse, terrorists trying to blow up the plane?

She placed her purse containing passport, money and medicine on a seat near the window on the row across and in front of her. She sat down as far away as possible by the opposite window—just in case. She took a deep breath: the plane taxied along the runway, then finally ascended. She sat rigid in terror during the whole flight. Her first flight ruined by her own stupidity. She'd dreamed of thrills, excitement: never of actual danger.

José Martí airport looked like an army base painted dull olive camouflage colours that merged into palm trees. The only thing in her memory that came close were World War II movies set in the South Pacific. After the plane halted on the runway, Amy walked across the aisle and gingerly picked up her purse. The steward opened the door: gusts of heat struck her. She trailed behind the missionaries, exiting by the front. Amy paused, staring, turning to look around in all directions. Everything was a dull green—hot, heavy and unreal. A group of toy soldiers marched towards the plane: with a twist of his shoulder, one pointed a gun indicating the direction she was to follow. Surprised, she halted briefly to notice that two of the soldiers had long hair. They were women wearing make-up. She remembered that her friend Elsie had been in the militia. Amy walked ahead obediently toward another set of soldiers and waited while the missionaries presented their documents, their luggage. She could see them inside a glass-enclosed cubicle. She watched a uniformed official behind a desk take his time inspecting their documents. She sweated, mopped her forehead, brushed her hair off her face. The soldiers smiled. One asked, 'Americana?' 'No,' she answered. 'Soy una Canadiense.'

'Muy bien!' he commented. She was trying to phrase a Spanish response when the cubicle door opened. The soldiers escorted the missionaries out through another exit. The soldiers escorting her motioned her ahead. She entered the room, presented her passport and permit to the official. In carefully-coached Spanish she lied, 'Estoy una amiga de la revolución,' just the way Elsie, who belonged to one of Walter's groups, and had 'served' in Cuba, had coached her to do. But not until after trying to persuade Amy to stay in Canada.

'You'll only be in the way,' Elsie had warned, 'but if you must go, you have to learn some important Spanish. Estoy una amiga de la revolución...'

'But I'm not a friend of the revolution, Elsie! I'm going to be objective.'

'Sure.' Elsie said. 'But to do anything you'll have to get around and avoid suspicion. Here's an address. It's a friend of mine, Martha Anderson. A teacher from Saskatchewan. She's fluent in Spanish—and is an official in the Ministry of Education. Knows people in high places.'

'I don't want anything like that,' Amy had retorted. 'I want to make it on my own.'

'You won't. You don't understand...' Elsie sighed, then continued.

'And another thing. Very important. They always sing *The International* after meetings. You'll probably attend some, hear the Spanish words. So for God's sake, sing, hum, whatever, or you'll offend the Cubans.'

'No way! I'd never sing *The International* in any language. Besides, I'm a foreigner. They won't expect it.'

'All the more reason. You're lucky you're even getting down there to visit at a time like this.' Elsie shook her head but thrust the card and the Spanish version of *The International* into her hand. 'Keep it. You never know. Okay, now. Once more. *Estoy una amiga de la revolución.*'

The officer rose, stretched across the desk and shook her hand, smiling. Two more soldiers arrived with her two suitcases, set them on a low table in front of his desk and opened both. On top; books, pamphlets from the consul, a Spanish dictionary. But from underneath the official picked up her silk fuchsia dress, fingered it, looked at her, as if imagining it on her, and said, '*Muy bonita. Muy bonita, señorita.*' He dropped it, slammed the suitcase shut, explored the other and motioned towards her shoulder bag. She shrugged it off and passed it across to him. Out came the Carpentier novel, and out came Amy's improvised Spanish. '*El está un autor muy bueno. El es Ministerio de Cultura. Verdad?*' The official eyed her purse, and there was murmuring in Spanish between the official and the soldiers. Shrugs. When the official reached out for her purse, she pretended to misunderstand

and quickly reached out to shake his outstretched hand, smiling.

'*Muchas gracias, señor. Je suis muy felice, también.*'

The soldiers chuckled, the officer nodded. He hesitated, shrugged, and released her hand. 'You speak excellent Spanish, *señorita*. I hope you will enjoy Cuba. You may go.'

Señorita. She smiled. A compliment, like being called *mademoiselle* in Quebec.

The soldiers led her to the *cambio* and waited while she exchanged traveller's cheques for Cuban pesos. Then they took her outside and summoned a taxi. One of the other soldiers leapt across the road to a border of foliage, plucked a flower, darted back and handed it to her. He smiled and touched her hair. The gesture was so sweet and Amy so exhausted that her eyes filled. Then he said in hesitant English, 'In my land there are no green eyes or golden hair.'

She breathed deeply, holding the waxy jasmine blossom to her face. She smiled at the soldier, too overcome by the scent, the moment, to speak. When she broke into a sob, he patted her shoulder.

An ancient Chevy rattled up. The driver took her luggage and held open the door.

She slid inside and leaned against the battered upholstery in relief. So far, just a gorgeous flower and gallant men. No exploding purse.

She collected herself as the driver started without any direction from her. 'Havana Libre,' she announced.

'No, *señorita. Vamos por El Tropicana.*'

She blurted in English. 'But I'm expected at *Havana Libre!* That's what I told all the officials!' The man shrugged. She repeated, '*Havana Libre, por favor!*' He drove along in the heat beside the ocean and she revived a bit, enjoying the ocean breeze. She craned her neck at the sight of enormous tropical flowers. Occasionally she held the jasmine blossom to her face and smiled. Eventually they arrived at a huge hotel. *El Tropicana.*

'No. *Señor, por favor, la hotel Havana Libré!*'

'No, *señorita,*' he said. '*Aqui.*'

'*Cuánto?*' she asked, and he answered, '*Nada.*' He was already opening the car door, and once she was out, he unlocked the trunk, grabbed her suitcases, slammed shut the trunk, and led her through the entrance and up to the desk. She had been told not to tip because Cubans did not like it, and now he wouldn't even accept a fare. She reached out and shook the driver's hand. '*Muchas gracias.*' The desk clerk did not intervene, just waited.

To her relief, the desk clerk spoke English. 'Please, may I see your passport and I will...'

'There's been a mistake. I planned to stay at the *Havana Libre!*'

'I know. But it is filled. This is a superior hotel, beside the ocean. You will enjoy it more here. There has been a change made especially for your convenience.' He pushed a pen and the form towards her.

Everything was so awful now, not like those sweet soldiers at the airport. Exhausted, hot, she wanted to scream. Something scary was going on. She'd heard that all the Commie-bigwigs stayed at the *Libre.* The kind of people from whom she'd hoped to get information for her article. Now they'd dumped her at this tourist trap. The clerk read disapproval on her face.

'*Havana Libre* is in the city! Here, you are on the *Malecón,* our famous ocean drive. This is much more luxurious for a visitor!'

Amy sighed, and finally took her passport from her purse and signed the register. The clerk summoned a tall man to carry her bags and said, 'At your floor, the police will examine your luggage.'

'Thanks.' She was sweating, her dress rumpled, but the many young men seated in the lounge smiled at her.

She was glad now of Elsie's friend, of having her address and phone number. The police would surely find the fake serum. She'd need all the help she could get to stay out of trouble. And she would demand a transfer to *Havana Libre*.

'*Está cansada?*' The man asked.

'*Si*,' she answered, '*Estoy muy cansada.*'

The elevator stopped at the ninth floor. The man led them towards the room. A policeman stood by the door.

'*Buenas tardes, Señora Campbell.*'

Gosh. Her name and everything. She was suspicious. They seemed to know all about her. The whole switch had been well planned. All this heavy intelligence stuff made her edgy.

The man opened the door and left after the officer set her suitcases down on the luggage rack. He opened both and rummaged around in them, carefully avoiding packages of tampons, lingerie. Then he asked, 'How long are you staying?'

'*Seis semanas. Más o menos.*' He picked up her shoulder bag, and she said, '*Soy una trabajadora social. Soy una amiga de la revolución!*' Then rushing to hold up the Carpentier book as a diversionary tactic, she said, '*El está un autor muy bueno!*' The policeman's face brightened, and he said in English,

'You read him in Canada?'

'Of course. Are you familiar with his work?'

'No.' The man turned to face her and said, 'If you have any problems, please report to the desk. We must keep you safe in our country.' He walked toward the door, nodded politely and left.

She wanted to shower, but she flopped down on the bed still clutching her jasmine. Now the scent was almost sickening because she was hungry, tired, and scared. She needed sleep. But she must decide what to do about the contraband bottle. She thought of her brother the lawyer. 'Obey the law of the land.' The policeman was nice. So what if it were a Commie police state? A foreigner was never above the law of the land, no matter what the land's politics.

She walked over to the sink, splashed water on her face, took a cologne bottle from her bag and squirted on *Joy* that Walter had bought her at Toronto duty-free. Then she left the room, walked to the elevator, descended, and strode calmly up to the desk.

'Do you need something? May I help you?' The friendly clerk again.

'Yes,' she said. Amy related her whole story of the men at Miami airport, the serum. She took the bottle from her purse and handed it to the clerk.

'There's a name on here,' she said, pointing. 'And a phone number. I'm very tired. I'm not sure what the correct procedure is. Would you please take care of it?'

'Of course.' He smiled a big open smile. 'Enjoy your visit.'

Now, Amy thought, I can finally shower, rest, change, and eat! Her panic left her, and she returned to her room. As she neared her door she heard the phone ringing. It must be a mistake, she thought. No one knows I'm here. The ringing did not stop until she unlocked the door, dashed across the room and picked up the receiver.

'*Buenas tardes*,' she said.

'Hello, you are Señora Campbell from Toronto?' The voice was anxious, impatient, but the English was clear and unaccented.

'Yes...'

'You have the medicine? For my sick child? My husband telephoned me from Miami. I phoned the *Libre* but you weren't there. I phoned all the big hotels until I found you. I've been desperate. My child. And besides, I thought you might like to have someone show you around.' Her voice sounded demanding, urgent.

Now Amy knew she had done the right thing. If this woman's child was so sick, why the offer to 'show you around.' It was some kind of trap, some trick. She waited.

'Mrs. Campbell?' The woman again.

'Yes, *señora*. I've left the medicine at the desk. You may pick it up there...'

Click. The woman hung up.

Damn. Nothing made sense. Amy opened her purse and searched for the card Elsie had given her. She dialled the number, got a receptionist who answered with an exuberant '*Venceremos*', but who could not understand Amy. After Amy repeated 'Martha Anderson, Martha Anderson' several times, a new voice finally announced, 'Martha Anderson.'

'Hello, My name is Amy Campbell? I'm from Toronto? I'm a friend of Elsie's. She suggested that I call you if I've any problems.'

'From Toronto? Tell me where you are staying, and I'll be right over.'

'*El Tropicana*. That's awfully kind of you, but perhaps I could just explain over the...'

'No. I'll be right over. Meet me in the lobby.'

'Thanks a lot. But how will you know me?'

Martha laughed. 'Easy. Goodbye.'

'Goodbye.'

Down in the lobby, Amy walked through the lounge and sat on an ornate stuffed chair among a group of chairs circling a glass coffee table. The desk clerk smiled and waved as she passed. There were still men of all ages lounging about. Suddenly she realized there were no women in sight. No wonder Martha knew she would recognize her. Feeling conspicuous now, Amy rose, walked over to a newsstand, bought a copy of *Hoy* and returned to her chair, hoping to hide behind it pretending to read. Male eyes followed as she crossed the floor. There were even guarded smiles. She caught the eye of a thin young man in khaki, and he seemed about to approach her when a short, stocky young woman burst into the lobby, spotted Amy, and darted across to her. She embraced her and blurted, 'It's so good to see someone from home! How's Elsie?'

'Great. Working hard. Causes. You know Elsie.'

'Yes. Now, what was your problem, Amy?'

Martha was plump and wore a simple beige cotton dress and sandals. Her skin was deeply tanned, emphasizing her bright blue eyes. She had taffy-coloured hair streaked blonde by the constant sun. Amy figured that she was a fair-skinned brunette whose colouring had been reversed in the tropics. Immediately she liked her, trusted her. There was a familiarity about her. She didn't look like some diehard Commie. Amy related her whole experience. The Miami men, the serum/heart medicine, the hotel switch, the frantic caller, the turn-over of the medicine, her thought about the 'law of the land.'

Martha beamed. 'You did exactly the right thing! It could have been drugs, an attempt to link you up with counter-revolutionaries, anything. I was alarmed at first, to hear of a Canadian woman coming here alone, and at this time. But you will have made a good impression reporting that incident. I wasn't sure what your connection to Elsie was...'

'I met her at Fair Play for Cuba. And I used to see her at other meetings.' Then Amy told Martha about her plan to write, to change her career. She did not tell her that she was fed up with social work—she didn't think it would go over too well with someone committed enough to a foreign revolution to leave Canada. Elsie had told her about long stretches of food shortages, of living on rice. Martha must have been really dedicated to stay on.

'I'm not sure what I want to write,' she told Martha. 'But the whole thrust in newspapers back home is of a possible attack on the U.S. by Russians here. I've been reading about the health care, nursery schools, and the alphabetization programme. One of those areas seems a better bet. I just want to get around as much as I can, talk to people, see what clicks.'

'Good. You are in luck.' Martha smiled. 'Would you be up to hearing Fidel speak tonight? There's an educational conference on. He's addressing it at the Chaplin Theatre tonight. At 9:30.'

'Really? Castro?'

'Really.' Martha scribbled something on the back of a card, handed it to Amy and said. 'Be ready at 9. I'll have you picked up right outside. Just show the driver this card.' She gestured toward the door by which she'd entered. Martha looked at her watch. She had become crisp, businesslike, but suddenly her face softened again and she asked, 'Are the leaves back home turning yet?'

'Just starting. Gosh, I didn't think you'd have time to remember things like that. You're so busy, and everything here is so beautiful. The tropics—I'm dazed.'

'Yes. But after several years one still misses the seasons.' Her eyes filled. 'I keep remembering the wonderful crunch of the first snowfall. But it's really autumn I miss most. The colours, the crisp air. And apples!'

Amy was surprised. She'd expected a bureaucratic type spouting rhetoric, and here was this homesick Canadian. Suddenly Martha said, 'I'll call you again and we'll get together. Have you had a meal yet? There's not much, really, but we have lots of avocados right now and they're great.'

'No, actually, I haven't had time to eat. I've been on the run ever since I got here. I want to explore. I've never seen tropical flowers before. The hibiscus flower is incredible, and the smell of jasmine knocks me out.'

'That's a typical first reaction to the tropics. I'm glad you like it here ... but after a long stretch, you'd miss Canada. You might be able to get enough information for several articles in a couple weeks. I'd advise you to do that. It is a tense time. Look.' She led Amy to the window. 'There's the Malecón— the road that stretches along the coast. Over there, the U.S. warship. Waiting.' She paused, pointing towards the opposite side. 'A Russian battleship. Ten days ago the U.S. battleship shelled the coast further down. Try to get your research done in two weeks and just go home. I'll give you any help I can. Call me, okay? Oh, and don't go out in the late afternoon. There's a downpour that time of the day. It's the rainy season, and you'd get drenched.'

'Oh ... whatever you say. Okay, I won't go out around four. But about going back so soon, no. I wanted to, you know, enjoy the ambience...'

'This is no time for that.' Martha's voice became brisk... 'If you want a vacation with ambience, go home and try another island.' Then, as if aware she had sounded irritable she added, 'It's hard for an outsider to understand. I mean, Amy, don't hang around down here unless you're prepared to join the militia.' She smiled, trying to make it sound like a joke. Amy remembered Elsie saying, 'You'd only be in the way.'

Martha reached out and hugged her, then held her by the shoulders and smiled. They were the same height, but Martha's energy, strength, and authority had given Amy the impression that Martha was taller. But then Amy knew she often felt that way about other people. That they were taller, when they weren't. It came from her own sense of inadequacy, this sense of smallness.

'Have a nap, Amy. And a shower. Hear Fidel tonight, then get back to me tomorrow. I can set up some meetings for you. The Women's Federation—Raúl's wife is president—

you'll like her. And some people from the Committee for the Defence of the Revolution. They're our self-policing neighbourhood groups. And of course, our nursery schools. So many women are back at school, taking jobs for the first time. That's worth writing home about.'

'That would be great. Thanks,' Amy replied. Martha's suggestions made her feel better. Trusted. They embraced again and Martha bolted out the front door.

Amy returned to her room and hung up her shirtmaker dress. The fuchsia silk would need to be pressed, and besides, she figured women here would dress simply, would have to in a post-revolutionary country. She might look too North American, too gringo. All Dressed Up.

She frowned. Her radio had evidently been turned on—Cuban music blazed forth. The beat was pleasing to her, but incessant, too exciting for her just then.

She showered, wrapped herself in a towel, turned off the radio and lay down on one of the two beds. There was an irritating hum coming from the radio. She must have just turned it down. She reached out. She had turned it off, but the hum persisted. She would mention this problem to the desk clerk later. She stretched out again on her bed, throwing off the towel and lying nude in the heat.

She dozed, tossed, awoke; dozed, tossed, awoke. No real sleep. Just a constant replay in her mind of the day's events. Kissing the kids goodbye, kissing Walter goodbye; the Miami episode; the near misses by Havana customs inspectors; the phone call. Disjointed episodes. Toronto—the morning, her family; Miami—officials, Cubans, and missionaries; Havana—officials, phone call, and Martha. By the fourth rerun, she grew restless, overcome by heat. Even the sheet beneath her was soaked in sweat. She felt torpid, unable to move.

Sounds on the street had gradually slowed down and vanished. Suddenly she heard an explosive drumming sound of a heavy downpour and her room filled with cool air. She savoured this cool air for about half an hour, gradually heard street sounds again. Quicker. As if the whole city were suddenly refreshed. She felt refreshed herself and smiled. She would hear Fidel Castro her first night in Havana. How about that! She saw herself telling people about it back home.

Elsie had been right about her needing a friend in Havana. Maybe she'd be right about learning the words to *The International*. Amy got up, reached for her purse from her dresser, and took out the typewritten sheet. If it hadn't seemed funny, she'd be really upset. Imagine me, learning these words. '*Agrupemonos todos*.' She said the words aloud, read the anthem again. And again. Then distraught, ripped the sheet into shreds and flung them into a waste basket. No!

She fell back on her bed, stretching. It's alright to cooperate with the law. To fit in. But there has to be a line drawn.

She rose, put on fresh underwear, decided against stockings, decided for heels, and put on her tired green dress. She needed make-up, eye shadow. It had amused her to see the gunslinging female militia soldiers with their bright green eye shadow, mascara, and lipstick. She was glad, for once, that she was a blonde, in this land where there were 'no green eyes or golden hair.' She sprayed on more *Joy*. She hesitated, then put on the white gloves. It was a Spanish country after all. Better to stick with little formalities; to create a good impression. She headed for the lobby.

It was crowded. Young people, mostly men, milled about talking, spilling into and out of the bar. She checked her watch. 8:30. My god, I haven't even eaten! She wondered if she had time...

'*Señorita*, may I offer you a drink?' A very black, very handsome man in a very white suit was beside her.

'I wouldn't dare. For one thing, I haven't time. I'm being picked up outside at 9.'

He smiled, 'I know. *Señorita* Anderson has arranged for you to hear Fidel. You are very lucky. But your car will be late, and it does not take long to drink a daiquiri. I am with the hotel. I know your driver will wait.'

'Daiquiris are my favourite drink. Are you sure I have time?'

'Very sure.' He took her hand and led her into the bar. He was better dressed than the khaki-clad young men in the bar whose loud chatter ceased as she entered. She stared at them. She noticed that the men walked with their arms around each other's shoulders. She'd meant to ask Martha about that.

'*Dos Papa Dobles!*' the man snapped.

'Oh, you've read Hemingway?' she said.

'No, I haven't. But we all know of him. He lived just outside Havana. Perhaps I could arrange for you to visit his old home.'

'Really? That would be marvellous!' A waiter scurried over and placed two huge frosted daiquiris before them.

'*Salud!*' said the man.

'*Salud!*' Amy sipped, then gulped while the man set his glass down. She glanced at her watch, and the man said, 'You've lots of time.' She was watching two men embracing. Her host chuckled. 'Believe me, they are *macho*. It is just the Latin way. We like to touch. It is not offensive.'

She felt embarrassed now for staring at the entwined soldiers. But soon she grew suspicious. She decided this man had been sent to make sure she did not hear Fidel. And how come he knew everything about her? About her meeting Martha, about her evening plans? Weird, unreal. She opened her purse, signalled to the waiter. Her host guessed her intent and smiled. He put his hand over hers and stopped her. 'You are our guest, *señorita*. I am the hotel coordinator.'

Angry, Amy thought a moment then said, 'Please, I'm independent. What do I owe you?'

'Nothing. One—you are in Cuba, and, revolution or not, we are still men. Two—I am employed by the hotel to ensure hospitality to our foreign guests. This is your welcoming drink.'

'Well. All right. Thank you. You've been very kind. But I am so worried I'll miss hearing Castro...'

'Fidel will not arrive until at least 10. He will speak for three hours, maybe four...'

'What! Won't people get bored?'

'Never! In fact, they will feel cheated if they do not get a long speech, believe me. Those who are invited are honoured. They would be insulted by a short speech.'

She shook her head, sipped her drink and smiled across at the man.

'Your English is perfect,' she said. 'You've no accent at all.'

'Thanks,' he said, and downed his daiquiri.

Amy followed, drinking hers quickly, 'This tastes wonderful.'

'Of course. The best white Bacardi, fresh limes. If you come back alone tonight...or if you come back, I'll order another for you.'

'Oh, I'll be back,' Amy said. 'I don't know anyone here. Except—'

'*Señora* Anderson. Who knows? You might make a new friend tonight, at the theatre.'

They both rose. He escorted her outside, and she was aware of smiles, whispers from the men in the crowded bar.

'Who are all those guys?'

'Students. From all over Spanish America. Columbia, Mexico, Venezuela, Chile. They have come to help build Cuba. They are serving in the army, but meanwhile attend school. A few of the older men are Russian, or from the Eastern bloc, *técnicos.*'

'Oh, I never knew about that. But why are they smiling? What's so funny?'

'One—you are the only woman here. Two—forgive me, *señorita*—but no one wears gloves in the tropics.'

At the entrance he said, 'I've other guests to attend to. There's a photographer from France arriving tonight. You'll excuse me?'

'Yes.' Redfaced, Amy thrust her gloves into her purse and leaned against the wall. She watched a green lizard dart out from some foliage across the opposite wall, and shivering at the sight, she moved away. Lizards were loathsome creatures. Well, the country and the flowers were beautiful. There had to be ugliness, too. Hidden, slithery things. She kept looking at her watch.

The guy in the white suit was right. It was 9:15 and still no car. Had the whole plan been another hoax? She was too confused, too tired to decide what to do. Take a taxi? Phone Martha?

Finally a jeep arrived. A handsome man in army fatigues called out, '*Señorita* Campbell?' She darted over to the jeep. He jumped down and opened the door and let her in beside him. When she handed him Martha's card he shrugged. She was confused. Was he a driver, or what? As if reading her mind, he smiled and said, 'I'm a friend of Martha's, Commandante de los Santos.'

He was really handsome. Slight, wiry, tanned, and easy-mannered. 'Friend of Martha's.' Lucky Martha. No wonder she stayed. Amy reminds herself, I am married. *Estoy casada.*

'*Gracias, commandante.*'

'My name is Rafael,' he said, and smiled, switching to Spanish. *'Está casada?'*

'No,' she said, 'I just had a nap.' The man frowned, looked confused, then smiled.

She remembered giggles in her Spanish conversation class, the confusion between *'cansar'* to be tired, and *'casar'* to be married. Now she blushed.

Once, Amy, in answer to 'Are you married?' had replied, 'I just had a nap,' and the class and the professor had laughed. She had smiled then but now her slip was not funny. She smiled awkwardly. Rafael noticed.

'Something is funny? No?'

'No, I'm just tired,' she said, and smiled even more, wondering what she would have answered in Spanish, wondering if her mistake had been deliberate, an unconscious slip to avoid telling him the truth.

'Martha says you are a friend of Elsie?'

'Yes.'

'She is well, Martha says. You also belong to the same...sympathetic groups?'

'Yes.' Well, she used to. No way. In spite of how kind everyone has been. Amy was already wondering about Martha's suggestion that she go home in two weeks. She remembered reading that a U.S. warship had really shelled the coast. There really were Russians here. And despite Walter, Elsie, Martha, and the handsome guy beside her, she did not feel that she was 'one of them.' She was a left-wing dropout. All the militarism here was scary, all the advance knowledge about her an indication of an intelligence system, of spying. She shivered.

But the tropics were thrilling. Her first foreign country, so gorgeous. She looked around on the drive, astonished by the exotic flowers. 'What are those?' she kept asking Rafael, and he replied, 'Hibiscus, jasmine, bougainvillaea.' Sometimes the air was heavy with puffs of scent. Jasmine and drama. Flowers and guns. Lizards.

'It's a gorgeous country!' she gushed.

'Yes, the tropics are seductive. And especially in Havana, the most sensual city in the world...' He was reading her mind again. What could she say?

He spoke again. 'Do you have any problems, Amy? Any questions?'

'Yes. It's a minor thing, but very irritating. The desk clerk will probably handle it. I can't seem to turn off my radio!'

Rafael chuckled. 'Really, you are wonderfully naive, Amy. I thought Elsie would have told you. All hotels are bugged — that's done through the radio.'

'Bugged? I thought that only happened in spy stories.'

'Amy, please. This country is in a crisis! Even Martha's activities are monitored, and she accepts this. She's a foreigner, no matter what her political affiliations are.'

'Oh.'

'So that means, querida, that you must be very prudent. No visitors. All will hear of it.'

'Oh.' She felt deflated, and dropped suddenly to reality again, but could not help wondering if even Rafael's home was bugged, and what he implied by 'visitors.'

Miffed, she said, 'I wasn't planning on any visitors.'

He smiled at that, as he slowed the jeep, parked it, but made no comment. There were crowds milling about outside the Chaplin Theatre. When they immediately parted to make way for Rafael, she realized he must be recognized as important, powerful. She could not differentiate ranks here. A commandante must be important. He kept his hand on her shoulder. Although comforted—she was afraid of crowds—she was vaguely disappointed. It was just the Latin custom. It meant nothing. He ushered her to the entrance and spoke briefly and quickly in Spanish to an official at the door, saluted her and said, 'Someone will drive you back. Perhaps myself. Wait here after the speech. Right here.'

'Thanks, Rafael.' He smiled. She smiled back. *Perhaps myself.*

NOW, seated all alone in the row marked *El Cuerpo Diplomatico do Canada* she wonders who will sit in the remaining eleven—she has counted—seats. Perhaps she will meet other Canadians, because Canada has maintained its embassy here. She keeps looking at her watch. Nine-thirty, nine-forty, nine forty-five. At nine-fifty the guards stand aside and a crowd rushes in to fill the vacant seats. What look like whole families head for the front rows. There is a group of women holding toddlers and babies who fill a row marked 'Los Estados Unidos.' Other Cubans smile as they join her to become instant diplomats of Canada. Now she is glad she wore the old dress because these new arrivals were simply and shabbily clad. But they are happy and excited.

There are sudden sounds of rustling; of bodies moving, and she hears 'Fidel, Fidel, Fidel' repeated in Spanish. Then the excited crowd is on its feet: chanting mounts, she hears 'Fi-del, Fi-del, Fi-del.' She is frightened, horrified, reminded of newsreels of Hitler during World War II. She wants to run, to leave the theatre, to head back to the hotel, back to Canada, home to Canada. There are sounds on the stage, and rustling up in front as armed militiamen appear in the wings.

He arrives. He stands less than seven feet away from her, up on the stage. Fidel Castro. The crowd is about to burst into an uproar. He holds up his hand and smiles. Like a priest, she thinks. There is immediate silence. A tinny loudspeaker plays what must be the Cuban national anthem. The crowd rises, but instead of standing at attention, the people are all joining hands, swaying as they sing.

Again, Amy feels terror. She shivers with chills in the heat. There is something so hypnotic about the music. She shakes her head, refuses to link hands. At the anthem's conclusion, the audience sits. A woman walks to the stage. Amy figures she is some educational official. The woman introduces one of the other men. The Minister of Education. He, in turn, rises and introduces Fidel. The chanting resumes and the audience is silenced again, by the smile, the raised priestly hand.

The auditorium is not air-conditioned, and now Amy feels sweat glue her dress to her back, which makes her doubly aware of how immaculate Castro looks. The creases in his trousers and shirt are crisp, sharp, and no matter how loudly he raises his voice, how passionate his rhetoric becomes—she has caught his frequent use of repetitive, parallel construction—he does not sweat. He is immaculate and cool. This surprises her—she had expected scruffy, sweaty, sloppy, the way he was pictured in American newspaper cartoons. But no. His voice is like music. It builds up to a crescendo, down to a diminuendo. The smiles of the throng are rapt. At first she tries to catch, to translate his speech in her mind, while he explains how many people have already learned to read in certain provinces, how many children started school, etc., etc., etc. Eventually she gives up, yields to the power of his voice, the rhythm of his speech. The sensation she feels is like that she felt fighting a current in a swift river when swimming—eventually allowing herself to be pulled with it. At intervals Fidel pauses, strides offstage to take a drink from an attendant, and before speaking again, makes eye contact with the audience. When he turns she can see his back muscles move under his shirt. His crisp dry shirt. There is a controlled finesse in his voice, his walk, his gestures, that is electrical. This, she knows, is charisma. Later she stops thinking, stops watching the rapt faces, the nursing mothers clutching babies to breasts.

Much, much later—hours later, his voice grows quiet. Then very gradually the pitch rises again until he concludes.

"Venceremos! Viva la revolución! Viva Cuba libre."

The crowd takes up the chant *'Viva Cuba libre!'* Amy rises with the crowd, stunned, but sees the beaming woman beside her. Now the loudspeaker is playing again, and the girls are distributing heavily-scented jasmine blossoms to each member of the audience.

Amy takes her blossom, lifts it to her face, drinks in the heavy scent. Again, a feeling of being trapped, lost, of needing to flee. When the woman beside her nudges, Amy responds automatically. Everyone is reaching out to hold the jasmine-clutching hand of each neighbour, making a huge floral chain. The woman offers her right hand to Amy. A man reaches across to her from the aisle, extending his hand to hers. She clutches her flower. Suddenly everyone is singing together, swaying, a human floral chain. Amy has become a link, and now has a sense of being somehow disembodied. Feels not sweat on her face, but tears. Now she hears a strong familiar soprano voice singing *The International* in unison with the swaying throng

> *...Agrupemonos todos*
> *En la lucha final...*

It is her own voice.

October 16, 1962
AMY waits at the bus stop. She looks at her watch, sighs, and shivers in Toronto's chilly October air. She's wearing her olive green shirtmaker, although it is cotton. For the memories. In spite of washings, she thinks it still smells of jasmine. She hunches her shoulders against the cold. But, she decides, it's not really that cold. It's just that I miss the tropics.

She remembers Havana, remembers leaving there, sobbing so uncontrollably that the two militia men escorting her had had to practically lift her onto the plane, patting her back like parents consoling a child, murmuring comforting words to her in Spanish.

She had been frightened, then, as well as grief-stricken. Frightened by the angry screams of *los gusanos*—worms—the rich Cubans fleeing to Miami. They shouted at Cuban airport officials, complained to customs officers while being searched, at having the linings of their clothes slashed open.

Martha had prepared her for this scene. 'There'll be confrontations at the airport. I have to explain it to you—it could look scary. Counter-revolutionaries and *los gusanos* have smuggled money out of the country in their clothes, and in Holy Statues. It looks ugly, but police searches have to be done.'

Then a hug. 'I hope you come back. You fit in. It's just that you must resolve things for yourself, back home. It's easy to get carried away, emotionally, in the tropics.'

She was, literally being carried away, lifted onto the aircraft by distraught soldiers. But all she took, besides her luggage, was a bottle of Bacardi for Walter, a pair of tiny gold stud earrings for Emma, and a child's book, in English, about Ché Guevara, for Sandy.

Amy had sobbed because she did not want to leave Havana, and, most of all did not want to leave Rafael. But it had been he, Rafael, who suggested that she leave. And, after she had agreed, he had personally arranged for her flight, and for militia escorts.

Only two nights ago she had been excited, as always, when he picked her up at the hotel and drove her along the Malecón, slowed down a fair distance from the hotel, and parked.

'Let's get out, *querida*, we must discuss something important,' he'd said. Then, sprawled close to her on the beach he explained with concern and urgency that she should reconsider her originally planned, two-month stay. The same advice she'd heard from Martha when she first arrived. But now, from Rafael, with greater urgency.

'If you remain,' Rafael said, 'and it would make me happy if you did—we will take care of you. You are improving your Spanish slowly. It will come. We will find something for you to do. Teach, perhaps. But it is possible that you might not be able to return to Canada for a long time, if you wait to leave in a month. If your children are important to you, you must leave immediately. This week.' He drew a long breath on his cigar, exhaled, and added, 'There may be problems.'

'What kind?' she asked, even though she knew well enough by then that when Rafael said little, she must not probe, must not ask questions. But her anguish at the thought of leaving broke her silence. 'Please, Rafael. What problems?'

'It is best for you if you don't know. Nothing is certain… so I am not free to discuss. All I can tell you, for now, is that if you wait, it may be impossible for you to leave.'

'I want to stay forever! But not until after I go home to bring back Emma and Sandy.'

'That may be possible later, but not now. If you stay on now, you might not see them… for a very long time.' He leaned forward, elbows on his knees, looking out to sea. Not touching her. She knew that if he touched her, right at that moment, that she would forget everybody, everything. That she would stay. At his side, hearing the ocean, smelling jasmine—Toronto, Walter, work, seemed unreal. But the kids...

'Come,' he said, sighing. 'I have work tonight, a meeting.' He did not even reach for her hand to lead her to the jeep. Once inside, both of his hands gripped the steering-wheel as he said, 'You know my feelings. You have been invited to remain. This possibility has already been discussed, been approved. But you must go inside right now. You must think about your children, and make this decision alone.'

Dazed, she did not look at him, did not reach out to him. He carefully avoided touching her while letting her out, and moved quickly away, leapt back into the jeep, into the driver's seat, showing no intention of escorting her to the lobby.

'I will see you tomorrow. We must act quickly, if you decide to leave.'

She looked up at him, stunned. Smothered a moan, then murmured, 'Goodnight.'

'Goodnight.'

For a moment she stood still, shocked and confused. Slowly she dragged her feet into the entrance. She wandered through the lobby, ignoring the usual greetings from students, the invitations for drinks. She headed to the elevator and waited. It seemed to take forever to arrive, forever to reach her floor.

In her room, she threw off her clothes, showered, then sprawled naked on the bed, thinking.

Emma. Sandy.

Before she left, Emma had cried because the dentist had informed her that she had to have braces. Emma balked, said she would refuse to wear them.

'I'll be back to take you to Dr. Blake,' Amy had promised. 'It'll be okay.' Then she thought, my God, Emma's on the verge of becoming a teenager. And those rocks in her dresser drawer, all neatly classified. Was she spending too much time with them, collecting, sorting, classifying? But kids were collectors—stamps, match folders, autographs. And she seemed to enjoy it so. Fingering a piece of rose quartz, she'd called, 'Come and look, Mom! Isn't it gorgeous!'

And what about Sandy? He can't get along with anyone at school, or anywhere else. If she didn't take him to craft classes, or sit for hours reading while he fished on Centre Island, he'd have no one. Walter was disappointed in Sandy. He'd wanted a hockey player and got a dreamer. And Walter, well, he was always away, and when he was in town, always out at meetings. Before, his absences enraged her. But now, in Havana, she is relieved. Her much-idolized Walter she viewed as a phoney, a mass of contradictions, a rhetoric-spouting bore. She sighs. Emma and Sandy. She must go back.

Within two days she was on the plane, huddled sobbing while *los gusanos* laughed and shouted, "*Viva Kennedy!*" They sneered at her for sobbing, frowned at her because of her preferential treatment. She hated them, wanted to throw something at them. The flight was a nightmare as her feelings swung from grief to rage.

AMY looks at her watch again. Paddy is late. Paddy her mentor who had encouraged her to write and taken her out for a drink and wanted to know all about her trip, all the details, asking dumb questions, but now not seeming to take her article seriously.

'I think I've got a real political story here, Pat,' she'd bragged. 'There's a sense of some coming emergency, the stuff about Latin American students, the year of alphabetization. I've enough for a whole series.'

'Scrap it. You're a beginner, girl. I've already spoken to the travel editor of *The Beacon*. A drinking friend. He's very keen on a travel piece. Forget the political stuff.'

'But that's why I went there! To find out! That was even your suggestion!'

'Pardon me. I thought you went because you wanted to break into journalism. You have to go with the market, girl. And travel, for now, it is. I've opened a door for you. Take it or leave it. And for the name of God, will you stop answering the telephone with that bloody *'Venceremos?'* You sound like a Commie.'

'That's how they answer in Cuba,' she'd asserted. "And if it's good enough for them, it's good enough for me. It'll do Canadians good to hear it. I always have to explain that it means, 'we shall conquer.' Sort of like 'we shall overcome'—"

'Jay-sus, girl, the sun down there has got to you. At least I hope that's all it is.'

Now he has had her story, *Magnolias and Machine-Guns*, for two days. It was easy to write the sort of feature he'd suggested. Play up the scenery, the men, the dancing. Why was he taking so long to read such a short piece? Because he didn't want to hurt her feelings? Worse, could he be rewriting the whole thing? The Mount Pleasant bus zooms north to the loop, which meant it would be back at her stop in eight minutes.

Amy fishes in her purse for a ticket, finds one, and clutches it between her teeth. She always has her ticket ready before the bus arrives. Sometimes she forgets she has done so, and takes out a second ticket for the bus driver. She ponders her reason for doing this. Chronic preoccupation with kids? With work? Fatigue?

She sees Paddy leap down the steps of his Glenforest home and sprint across the street on a red light. She always marvels at this heavy man, with his terrible habits, making such speed with safety and ease.

As he bounds toward her, he beams, patting his briefcase, and greets her with an unexpected hug.

"What's that for?" she asks.

"Your smashing suntan," he said. "And your golden hair and green eyes. And this nifty little travel piece. Has Ed phoned you yet?'

'Ed?"

"*The Beacon* travel editor. He loves your story."

Amy tingles. "Really?"

"Yep. And the good news is, he wants to use it pronto, and you'll be paid on acceptance. Isn't that great?" He waits.

"Paddy, what's the bad news? Come on."

"Just some minor changes, love. That's routine even for staff writers. Editors like to do that. Get used to it. Ed wants to talk to you. He thinks it's still too political. He wants the crisis thing played down, romance and dance played up. And the title changed."

"But it's a beautiful title! No, never. I won't change it. Not for *The Beacon*, that Tory rag."

"Amy, you're a damned fool. They'll pay you two hundred dollars as soon as Ed gets your revision. Ed's a travel editor. People only travel for landscape, romance, and fun. The machine-gun title would scare them off. Ed will call you. Here's your piece. It's a good first effort, but there are dozens of those on his desk every day. You've an advantage if you take it, because right now Cuba is hot news, and the whole paradox about it being a great place to vacation with all this talk about a crisis, gets your foot in the door. Change the title, cut out the crap about police searches and bat-tleships and you make yourself two hundred dollars. Maybe you'll even land another assignment. Travel editors can do that. Pay for another trip. If you're cooperative. But you know, I sense you're keeping something back. We'll go for drinks. You can confide in your pal Paddy."

Amy was distressed, but encouraged by the thought that if she rewrote and cooperated, she might be asked to do more assignments. And she resented Paddy's intrusion, his personal questions. What happened in Cuba was sacred, not to be shared.

The bus stopped in front of them. They climbed on and Amy dropped her ticket in the box, clutched her story and slid it into her briefcase along with her clients' files and a copy of *The Canadian Social Worker*. Pretty soon, she thinks, I'll be transferring my clients, writing full time and travelling all over. Where? Guyana? No. She smiles. To Havana. A follow-up. A series...

She is humming *Besame, Besame Mucho* to herself, but stops abruptly when she hears Paddy chuckle. She keeps singing it to herself at home.

"There's more went on down there than you're telling. I'll find out." With that, and a smug grin, he bounds to the front of the bus and leaps off.

RAFAEL. Rafael. She writes to him daily, no replies. She writes to Mercedes, his sister. Nothing.

At work she moves through the day in a dream, declines lunch with co-workers Marnie and Joyce in order to work on her article. These two have always been smug and condescending towards her. Now it's her turn to get even.

"Sorry," she says. "My editor said he'd be calling."

"How exciting," Marnie says. Joyce smirks.

Amy thinks, wait until they see my byline.

Ed McNaughton does call. The curious secretary, Marge Hutton, always grills male callers, and is impressed. She scampers into Amy's office and opens the door.

"It's *The Beacon*, for you. Line three."

"Thanks," Amy responds. Marge lingers. But Amy waits, getting the most out of the moment. "Will you close the door when you leave, please, Marge?"

"Will do." Slam. Amy picks up the receiver.

She is about to proclaim, *'Venceremos!'* But instead, she pauses and says, "Amy Campbell."

"Hello there, Amy. I like your little piece on Havana that Paddy showed me. I like it so much, in fact, that I'm rushing things. I want your revision back by tomorrow at the latest so we can set it up to go into next Thursday's travel supplement. I'm pulling out another story so I can use yours. Did Paddy discuss the rewrite?"

"Sort of. He mentioned something about a new angle… cutting out a few bits."

"Yeah. The hard stuff. Guns, battleships. More dancing and daiquiris, get it? And the title has to go. I'll work on that myself. Not to worry. Okay?"

Amy hesitated. Ed broke the silence. "I suppose Paddy told you that our policy was payment on acceptance. I'll authorize your cheque as soon as I've edited your rewrite."

That did it. Two hundred dollars would almost pay for a return flight to Miami, and she'd find a way to pay for the Havana trip herself.

A client phoned to cancel her afternoon appointment. What great luck. Instead of working on her records, Amy put on her glasses, squinted, pulled out her story and laid it on her desk.

She centred the paper and retyped, cutting and adding as she went along. Got rid of some Russians, Rafael's military history, and her very private unpolitical meeting with Fidel.

She read and reread, crossing out some passages, adding others. Then she typed:

Amy Ryan
1714 Mt. Pleasant Drive
Toronto, Ontario

Magnolias and Machine-Guns

For me, a Canadian tourist in Havana last month, the city was a place of paradox and rhythm.

When I stepped off the plane I caught sight of drab army trucks and deep green palm fronds—my first encounter with the military and the exotic, with the political and the poetic.

I stayed in the luxurious hotel *El Tropicana*—a mammoth curved skyscraper, once a Batista playground. It was decorated with potted palms, abstract paintings, deep rugs, and low marble tables. On these tables were ashtrays painted with Spanish slogans urging workers of the world to unite.

Just as in days of the old regime, here guests sipped daiquiris, swam in the pool by day, and danced to Latin music at night. They danced the mambo, the tango, the cha-cha-cha. So did I.

But now the guests were Latin American students, here "to work for the revolution," and before entering the ballroom for a Saturday night fiesta I passed a sign which proclaimed in Spanish that it was prohibited to carry guns onto the dance floor.

Relationships were egalitarian. My chambermaid embraced me and called me *compañera*; the bell-hop shook my hand and called me *camarada*.

Because there were few women, and no North Americans staying at *El Tropicana*, I always had for companions the gallant Latin American students to escort me around Havana.

I was fortunate to meet, on the evening I arrived, Commandante Rafael de los Santos, who became my friend, protector, and tour guide. Although he had attended the same Jesuit school as Fidel Castro and had fought at his side in the Oriente hills, he did not fit the stereotype of a revolutionary. He enjoyed Beat poets, French playwrights, Russian novelists, and Cuban rum. He was exotically handsome, and his face, with slanting dark eyes and sloping cheek-bones, reflected the mixture of which he was so proud—Arawak, African, Spanish and Portuguese. He had attended the University of Mexico where he studied social sciences with Erich Fromm, before returning to Cuba to finish his medical training.

We walked miles together, through the narrow balconied streets of old Havana, where we drank tiny cups of sweet, dark Cuban coffee; along the sea wall, where he taught me to sing the old songs of the Spanish Civil War; and through the residential district of Miramar where we admired Creole mansions with their tangled gardens of hibiscus, jasmine, and oleander.

Besides Rafael and the students who befriended me, there were the endearing Cuban people. Most of them served in the militia, but their duties would never let the possibility of an attack tomorrow spoil the pleasure of a fiesta tonight.

My first encounter with the poetic Latin men occurred when a soldier, escorting me from the airport to my taxi, observed me admiring tropical flowers.

He darted away and returned to hand me a cluster of jasmine. In careful English, he said, 'In my land there are no green eyes or golden hair.' Then, still carrying his machine-gun, he resumed his military sense of duty.

I grew very close to Mercedes, little sister of Rafael. Sixteen, sultry-eyed and sensuous, she drove a tractor at volunteer farm work. Her only wish was 'to work for the revolution.' She generously befriended not only homesick Latin-American communists, but this solemn Canadian tourist. 'Don't be lonely, chico,' she cooed to the Venezuelan lad. 'Come on, smile, have fun, North American,' she demanded of me.

I declined her parting gift of a medal picturing the Kremlin. 'It looks so nice on you,' she said. I hedged. 'Okay, okay, so you won't wear it,' she laughed. 'I understand.'

Two of her brothers lived in the United States and criticized the revolution. Two others had fought for Castro and were slain in the Oriente hills by Batista's men, had their eyes and fingernails torn out. 'I can't stand it at home,' she told me. 'My brothers' pictures are everywhere, and they make me sad. But Rafael and me, we stick together.' And so she came to *El Tropicana* each day, to cheer us up.

Rafael explained that these students with whom I talked and explored Havana belonged to what has been termed "The New Elite." Hand-picked by Communist leaders in their own countries, they had been invited to Cuba to study, and to meet Castro's need for professional and technical personnel. They received from the Cuban government tuition, books, clothing, room and board. Before moving to student residences at universities, they were guests at luxury hotels.

I expected these students to be dogmatic, hard-headed, regimented. But they surprised me. After attending a propaganda film on the Chinese Revolution with them, they had sneered. 'What a terrible picture! I wish Cuba had the dollars to import some decent French, Italian or Swedish films,' said one. Another added, 'Yes. I am a Communist, but those Russian movies: Nothing but work and war, war and work!'

Rafael took me to the bar where Hemingway drank, to the home where Hemingway had lived and worked: showed me Hemingway's books, his chair, always with a knowledgeable running commentary, indicating his familiarity with the author. 'Manic-depressive,' he said, with a shrug. 'So sad.'

I did not want to leave Havana—its music, its people, its rhythm. Because above all, I remember Havana for its rhythm.

Even the weather had a rhythm which in turn gave a score to one's day. In early morning heat, people and buses moved slowly to work; by oppressive torpid noon movements dragged down, many offices closed, and those workers who could, slept. Until late afternoon heat piled on heat, throbbing, building up until the sudden climax of rain splashed down in sheets, sending laughing pedestrians scurrying for shelter from the downpour.

After the rain ceased, the air was cool and light: peoples' steps quickened, and the bright little lizards that slithered along garden walls puffed out their throbbing orange throats with joy. From then until early morning one could work, dance, sing, argue, walk, make love.

Always too, there was the rhythm of music—of conga, rumba or tango — beat out on two sticks by a dark boy on a bus as he made up songs for amused passengers; banged on steel drums by a laughing rum-drinking group at the beach; or strummed on guitars at a midnight fiesta.

My last evening in Havana I spent as I had the others. Dancing with Rafael. I was confused, when I finally made out a familiar tune played as a tango, and laughed when I realized it was "Moscow Nights."

'If you think that's funny,' Rafael said, 'you should hear the dock workers singing *The International* as a cha-cha-cha.'

After I returned to Canada the reinterpretation of the Communist anthem seemed symbolic, for I had learned that whatever Cuba borrowed from the U.S.S.R.—be it ideology or music—it would become distinctively Cuban in its meaning and rhythm.

Indeed, at first I admit to being alarmed to hear *The International* sung at large gatherings. But now, knowing as I do, the new Cuba, for me the anthem has lost its revolutionary meaning and become another joyous Cuban hymn of celebration.

For this was Havana, in September, 1962.

————30————

THERE. That should do it, Amy decides. But she feels a sense of loss, cutting out the drama, the danger, the intrigue. The smuggled drugs, and especially the Russian and American battleships always ominously in the harbour, because in her first draft she'd played up the *Dover Beach* aspect. But Ed's notes said it emphasized the crisis. 'Chuck this,' he'd written in the margin. She sighed, remembered facing the ocean and quoting, 'Oh love let us be true to one another.' Only to hear Rafael add, 'for the world, which seems so various, so beautiful, so near, hath neither joy, nor love, nor light. Nor certitude, nor peace, nor help for pain, and we are here as on a darkling plain swept with confused alarms of struggle and flight where ignorant armies clash by night.'

Rafael. She fights tears. Stop! She straightens up at her desk, slides her story into her briefcase before tackling the correspondence that had accumulated during her vacation. Requests for case histories, for reports. Finally she returns these to her file drawer and locks it. Usually she never got out the door at closing-time, but tonight she senses she can bet on Marge's curiosity.

She strides out of her office at 4:45 and says, "I have to leave early, Marge. I'll make it up tomorrow. *The Beacon* is demanding this article."

"Then get going dear," Marge beams.

Amy hates it, the patronizing way Marge calls the social workers, 'dear.' A way of pulling rank. And she wonders why it is that wherever she, Amy Ryan Campbell, has worked, the secretaries were the real bosses. They called all the shots and the so-called professionals, the supervisors, were just powerless peer consultants.

"Thanks, Marge," she replies, just as Marge darts into Joyce's office. To report, Amy thinks, on my journalistic jaunt.

Outside, Amy jumps onto a passing streetcar, shuts her eyes until she senses from sounds that the tram has neared downtown. She opens her eyes, watches for her stop, looks forward to completing her errand, to getting home. Maybe there will be a letter today. Sandy will be waiting, watching out the window. But Emma seems to have changed, grown apart. Always on the telephone now, or reading up on The Beatles. Had my trip, our separation done that? Is it my fault, Amy wonders? No... teenagers! I hope.

She strides into *The Beacon* building and hands her story to a security guard. "Ed McNaughton is expecting this," she announces. "Right away."

"Right away," the guard says, and disappears to drop it in a slot. "It'll be up there in half an hour."

The next morning, Ed phones her. "Nice little story, Amy. It's to go in next Thursday, October 22. I've not only already authorized your cheque but I've come up with a catchy new title—*Cha-cha-cha si, Crisis no.*"

"Oh, but I thought..."

"It'll look great. Have fun with the cheque. I'll keep you in mind if another assignment comes up."

"Great. Thanks," she announces, and hangs up. Marge enters.

"What did McNaughton want? Did he dump your story?"

"No," Amy says. "He's using it next week. And get this, I've already been paid. Two hundred dollars, and he says he's going to give me more assignments. I suppose I'll wait until later, before I formally resign."

"Nice. You know, I've always thought about writing. Articles. Romance novels. Now I think I will."

Amy wanted to pick up something, to throw it at her.

"Do that," she says, and sees a gleam of triumph in Marge's eyes.

It is hard for Amy to return to work, to remember the tangled lives of her clients, but it is better than being at home.

Walter is driving her nuts. He keeps bragging about her political experiences to his friends as if they were his accomplishments. He expounds on her journalistic career and her new political awareness. But privately, he tells her, 'Cool it, Amy. What would the department think?'

And, once a morning person, Amy now feels lousy in the morning. Just some tropical bug, she hopes. But there is her article to look forward to and her exciting new career as a journalist.

Editor's note:

Amy Campbell received her cheque, although her story was pulled from The Beacon *near midnight, October 21, on the eve of the missile crisis. An enraged Ed McNaughton had awakened her with the brutal news. Distressed by this, she began staying up late at night drinking rum and listening to all-night newscasts, until she learned of her pregnancy.*

Walter, who had wanted another child, was delighted.

Amy spent her two hundred dollars on maternity clothes and continued to practice social work until April 23, 1963, when she gave birth to a son. The eight pound, ten ounce boy was registered by Walter as Ernest Fidel Campbell.

Walter Campbell received a large inheritance in the mid-1970s which enabled him to leave his work as a civil servant in Toronto. When Amy refused to join him in a vegetarian commune he was organizing near Kapuskasing, Ontario, he arranged for his youngest son, Fidel, to attend Upper Canada College.

Amy Campbell remained in Toronto with her two older children and resumed her social work career until Emma and Sandy were grown and established. Her daughter, Emma Campbell, studied geology at the University of Toronto and now lives in Inuvik.

Sandy Campbell was one of the first male students admitted to the National Ballet School. He lives in Paris where he is a dance choreographer.

Ernest Fidel Campbell visited Cuba once with his mother, as guests of the Cuban government, to attend a memorial ceremony honouring Cuban casualties in Angola, where Commandante Rafael de los Santos was killed in action in 1975. Ernest had his name legally changed to Ernest Walter Campbell before leaving to attend Harvard. He is a corporate lawyer and lives in Boston. He is now a U.S. citizen.

The two evangelists were CIA agents.

Paddy O'Donnell was an RCMP informer and wrote a bestseller about his experiences following the MacDonald Inquiry.

Amy never did find out what was in the bottle she had carried from Miami to Havana.

Amy Campbell received a fellowship to study linguistics at the University of Michigan in 1980, but was refused admission to the United States. She subsequently moved into St. Ann's Gaelic College in Cape Breton, Nova Scotia. After learning Gaelic she moved to Scotland and now resides in Aberdeen, where she is active in the Scottish Nationalist Movement.

bell curves

I GRAB my passport and handbag. I'm rushing, because I want to catch the travel agent this morning so I can nab a charter to France. Should I leave May ninth or sixteenth? May ninth.

The telephone. Damn. I don't need another delay. I hesitate because I'm in such a hurry to leave. But I'm curious. I can never leave a telephone unanswered. It might be my daughter Margaret, or her long-gone brother Andrew, or that horny poet from last week's Harbourfront reading. Oh!

"Hello," I say. It sounds hollow. Someone's calling long distance.

"Hello? This is Peggy Sweeney? Tim Mulligan's sister? Are you Alice O'Connell?"

"Yes."

"Thank God! I'm calling from Baltimore. This is an emergency—about Tim? I tried Mike McKernan first. He gave me your number, and told me I should call you because you live near Tim. I'm frantic. I know we've never met, Alice, and I wouldn't call you if Tim hadn't told me all about you, but I feel I know you. That you're a friend."

Mike McKernan. Married to Maureen, Tim's former girlfriend. Painters. But Tim? What could he have told her about me?

"Well not exactly a friend, but yeah, I take care of his studio sometimes. What can I do for you?"

"Tim was supposed to arrive in Baltimore at midnight. He never got here. I was going to give his licence number to the police here, but I thought I'd better try up there first. Try to find out if anyone knew anything. You see, Tim's been having car trouble. When he never arrived I could just see his body spread out on the highway."

"If he had car trouble maybe he took a bus," I suggest, looking at my watch. "Maybe he'll be in later by bus. Or maybe, Peggy, he just changed his mind."

There. That should reassure her. Soon I'll be off, on my way.

"He'd have phoned. That's another strange thing, Alice. He always phones before he leaves, so I know something is terribly wrong. He'd never change plans, because this is a very special weekend for our family. You see, I saved up all my weekends to have this one off for Tim. I'm a nurse. Mother is coming in from New York. Tim knows this. His own mother is coming and we're all to be together for Kathleen's graduation."

Oh yeah, the niece. Now I remember. I stayed at Tim's studio once when he went to visit her.

"Kathleen, Tim's niece? Your daughter? The redhead? Tim is crazy about your children, Peggy."

"His surrogate family, Alice, let's face it. And my kids think there's no one like their Uncle Tim. The boys are into baseball now, so they're kept busy. Involved. Tim told me all about you. You're the painter around the corner who works in his studio when he goes away."

"Not really a painter. I'm just a beginner. It was another night school teacher—a friend of Tim's—she teaches printmaking, who told me that Tim often went away and needed—"

"Right. A studio-sitter. But listen, Alice, we've been up all night waiting. I'm frantic, and Kathleen's saying the rosary.

Dear God, what if there's been an accident? What if his body is lying out in a ditch? What if he's sick? Maybe that's why he never phoned. Have you seen him?"

"As a matter of fact, I have, yes. Two days ago on the street. He looked great. I don't remember him saying anything about Baltimore."

"He never even mentioned this trip? Has he forgotten his family? I can't believe it! Poor Mother. She'll be seventy in May. We've planned it for months."

There is a pause. I look at my watch and hear, "Did he look depressed? There's lots wrong with Tim, you know. Ever since he decided to be an artist instead of a priest."

God, I think, and grab a kitchen chair. I slide it towards the phone and plunk down on it. She's one of those Irish talkers. This is going to take a while. Unless I can think of something to head her off, I'll be lucky if I get to the travel agent's before my husband Billy wakes up.

Reassurance should do it. Lots of reassurance and she'll hang up. After all, it is long distance, and it's her nickel.

"He looked great," I exclaim. I've never seen Tim look so well. But then, I hardly ever see him. As I started to explain, Peggy, I'm just a beginner in a night school class. He's an artist. He's doing so well that he's got a real dealer and everything. All the other students at this community college where he teaches speak highly of him. But no, I don't see a lot of Tim. As I said, one of the other teachers, Tim's friend, told me I could use his studio when he went to New Mexico that time. I was a bit in awe about the whole thing. Tim's studio. But no, we never visit. Tim only sees me if there's some arrangement about his going away. Being an artist, he needs privacy. Space—"

"Space! That's Tim. Always going on about space! One of his worst problems. And this idiocy about no telephone. God forbid, what if Mother died? Or I was sick? Or if he was sick? He'd just lie there with no way of us knowing."

"I can understand the phone part," I said. And by now I really did. "No interruptions."

"He could get an unlisted number," Peggy continues. "Do you have them up there in Canada?"

"We do." Also hot and cold running water, I want to add.

"Alice. You've got to do me this one little favour. As a friend. As a dear friend. Go to his place and find out if he's left. Make sure he's all right. I'll phone later, okay?"

"Okay. About an half hour? I'll bang and bellow. If there's no answer I'll slide a note under his door. He doesn't always answer his door if he's working."

As soon as I've said it, I'm mad at myself. How do I let myself get my day ruined like this? I planned to get out this morning, to book my flight, and avoid having to listen to my husband Billy.

"I know that," Peggy chirps. "He won't even answer his door. Isn't that the limit? Have you ever heard of anything so crazy? Please hurry, Alice. Make sure he's not sick—lying in there. I'll call again—in forty-five minutes. Exactly. Forty-five minutes. Okay?"

"Okay. Goodbye, then, Peggy."

Forty-five minutes! Goddamn! My charter! But do I really want to go to France? With my pea-soup accent? They'll hate me. But I'll get away from Billy, get my own space. I sprint out the door.

It's a fast getaway or my marriage. Billy and his cigars; me raging at Cuban fumes knowing his chain-smoking episodes precede weekends at Greenwood Racetrack. We should talk, Billy and I should, but whenever I try to discuss our problems he just won't listen. Just smokes away dreaming of wealth; or launches into totally irrelevant lectures on the Bell curve, modems, and fourth dimensional mathematics, which all emerge from clouds of Tuero smoke. All stuff I don't understand, but enough to distract me from discussing his gambling. When I try to explain, I get 'Did Edison's wife nag? Did Einstein's? I'm on to a system as brilliant as anything those guys dreamed up.'

Bell. Thank God for Alexander Graham. The curve has soared on the long distance bill. Calling friends. They listen. Friends do not lecture me about statistics; do not promise me a fortune, a rosy future. Nor do they smoke cigars. At least, my friends don't.

Our daughter Margaret understands. She should. She's a social worker. And she knows her old man. Took one look at me during a recent visit and announced, 'Mom, you're exhausted.' She went home and got on the Bell (the phone, not the curve), and came up with a place for me in Normandy. Le Havre. Some friend of hers needed a chateau-sitter.

'Like Braque, Dufy, Matisse,' she said. 'You know those guys, Mom. Those whatchamacallems.'

'The Fauve artists,' I sighed.

'Maybe you'll even paint something.'

'I have painted something.' Several dozen water-colours, and the bathroom walls. And two of my water-colours were even chosen for the college student exhibit. 'I can't afford the flight,' I told her. 'Not yet. Later, maybe. Your father says I can travel anywhere I want, once he starts winning.'

That day she phoned I'd thought Billy was in his computer room working on the handicap stats, but he has this uncanny ability to intrude at crucial, private moments. Like an Irish nun.

From his study door, Billy had been listening to me on the phone and was beside me in an instant. He immediately interrupted—'I'll take care of it. Why wait when I'm on to a sure thing? It'll be good therapy for you. You've never faced your bicultural heritage, your shaky identity. All you

Canadians have shaky identities. The trip will resolve all that. Get you in touch with your French history. Canada's first settlers came from Normandy. Besides, it'll be better for me with you gone. I'm busy working on the spread sheets for my betting system. With you away I'll have privacy, more time to concentrate.'

'Identity? My identity is firmly British Columbian. The Kettle Valley. I'm a Westerner.' I've fallen into his trap, let him confuse the issue the way he always does. And all this while Margaret was yelling into the phone, 'Mom? Are you there? Tell Dad to shut up!'

'That's why you should go to France,' Billy insisted. 'The Western separatists are a bunch of rednecked racists. Go to France, girl. You'll see. You'll love it. Who knows better than myself who's travelled there? The wines, the cheese, the races. Great breeders there. Great talkers, like yourself.'

'But my French ,' I protested.

'Right. Your French is worse than Diefenbaker's was. But you do need to get away. What you should do is take the ferry across to Ireland and see my family. It'll keep them off my back and affirm your own Irish identity.'

'Mother!'

'Yes, Margaret. Sure. Sounds good. Great in fact. Better and better. I'll call you back.'

I hung up and continued to argue with Billy. As usual.

'I'm my father's child, Billy. A Scot. They believe in work. And with all the packing and travel I'll never get ready for an advanced class. But I've nothing against a trip to France. I might do some new work on my own.'

'Work? Work is for losers. Go to Ireland too, like I said. Ireland will do wonders for your self-esteem. Here you seem crazy, but in Ireland you'd find that everybody is just like you. Always talking. You'll come home with an okay feeling about yourself. Now the Irish—'

'The Irish be damned. I know about their talking. But also that they're all drunks and gamblers!'

No way would I visit his bloody family, who write and send me Mass cards and blessed medals. No mention, that day of his sister, the gambling nun; of his other sister, the white witch of Wexford.

But, France, now. Normandy. New seascapes, new colours, different light. Artists are always going on about light.

A trip abroad might open me up. As an artist. I might enter a whole new period, the way Picasso kept doing. I'd experiment, away from teachers and bloody Toronto and home and Billy. I'd take a young lover—French or Spanish— thin, dark and intense. I'd know what real lovemaking was like again. God, how long has it been? Anyway, he'd open me up emotionally, this young man, and I'd burst out of pastels into blazing colours. In the morning, he'd be tired, and lie about while I used him for a model, nude. I'd make us *café au lait*, go out picking wild flowers and decorate his penis—No they'd fall off. I'd make garlands and drape them around it.

He'd be very jealous of other men, my Frenchman or Spaniard, and mad about me. Young Frenchmen prefer older women, women of a 'certain age,' they call it. Experienced. That writer, Colette, that's what she did and it worked for her. Did her wonders.

When I returned my new paintings would cause a sensation. All the trendy dealers—those new ones down on Spadina—would be after me. I'd have a real *vernissage*, with bigtime reviewers from *The Globe and Mail* and *The Star*. They'd give me rave reviews, unlike the snide lines in *Here*, a Toronto tabloid that covers arts and 'alternative lifestyles.' Of my water-colours in the student show the reviewer wrote, 'Water-colours that might have been painted by your Aunt Martha, or at the most, be suitable gifts for Aunt Martha.'

They were wonderful water-colours. Zucchini, eggplant and onions. I called them *Ratatouille 1 and 2*. Really original.

In France I'll move out of my vegetable period...

At the opening, the real one, when I got back, there'd be red SOLD stickers on all my paintings of my naked lover. *Flowers on Phallus* would be bought by the National Gallery. I'd be invited to exhibit in New York and Philadelphia, be banned in Cleveland. Feminists would picket and reviewers would write, 'Never has the male body been so gloriously celebrated.'

Well, I'd be all alone, anyway. With no laundry, no meals, no racing forms all over the living room. I might even work in a side trip to Paris and visit the Louvre. And drink wine. A lot of wine. With the young Frenchman, or the moody Spaniard.

And get away from the phone, too, like Tim. Tim! Dear God, I almost forgot Tim! Just standing here by the phone, dreaming.

How could Tim be sick? Tim the non-smoker, herbal tea-drinker, meditator? I'd spent enough time in his studio to learn his habits. Health foods, exercise equipment; books on nutrition and Buddhism. Calcium tablets, I'd noticed guilti-ly, as I popped a Valium.

A night person, Tim. Myself, mornings. Lucky for Peggy Sweeney, whose Baltimore call already had taken up a half hour of my precious early day. I lace up my running shoes and spring out the door, leap down the steps, turn the corner to head for Dufferin Street and into the old brick warehouse, then along the hall to Tim's. They are all late sleepers in this building. I knock. Rap. Rap-rap-rap. RAP-RAP. BANG.

"Tim? Tim, it's Alice." I hate this. But now I'm account-able to Peggy, Kathleen, the baseball nephews, and his mom, seventy in May. Usually I knock gently, stand outside, listen-ing for rustling paper, running water, heaving bedclothes, breathing; know when to leave after an unanswered knock. Know when he is in there wanting to be alone wearing his Japanese cloak, stirring macrobiotic foods in a wok, performing various bodybuilding and spiritual exercises. Making love? Artist's models always sleep over. Always. Mine will. He'll move right into the chateau.

Tim's not in there, not in his flat. I can feel it. I go around outside and bang on his window. If he were in there wanting to be alone, even my banging would do no good. He'd ignore it. But this time at least I can tell Peggy I tried.

I dig in my purse for paper, and find an envelope. A pen? None. Lipstick. Cover Girl persimmon red will catch his eye. On the envelope I write:

PEGGY CALLED. FRANTIC.
EXPECTED YOU LAST NIGHT.
CALL HER!! ALICE.

I slide it under his door. Now I will be able to tell big sister I tried everything.

What about his car, I wonder, and sprint around to the back. There it is in the parking lot. His battered maroon Mazda. He never even left. He is not splayed out on a Maryland highway. Good news for Peggy. Now I'll have some peace, and finally be able to get downtown to book my charter.

I rush home to await Peggy's call. As I leap up the steps, through the picture window I can see Billy reading the racing form and smoking a cigar. Not drinking coffee, not eating the morning-fresh croissants I rush out to buy him early Saturdays. I hear Nana Mouskouri singing in French. An omen, that, surely, although usually I resent her because Billy's heavy smoking episodes are always accompanied by his precious tapes of Nana singing in French, German, Greek. But she doesn't make me jealous this morning. I'll have my

Frenchman, or my very own Spaniard. A Basque... Today Billy is asking for trouble, breaking an unspoken rule. No smoking in the living room. Ordinarily, we'd have had a row, but now thoughts of my new lover, my new paintings, my rave reviews, all sweeten my mood.

I burst in. He frowns. He thought I was gone for the day, or if not, would give him hell. He turns on the charm. "Good morning, lass. Enjoying the fine day?" So nice-nice. Yes, he's going to the racetrack.

Nana persists. *Chan-ter la vie...* French. It's an omen for sure. It was all meant to be.

"Pardon me if I disrupt your morning musical interlude with the racing form, but I have to wait here for a long distance call...from Baltimore. Tim Mulligan's sister Peggy phoned. Tim was expected there last night and never arrived..." I wave away cigar fumes and wrinkle my nose.

la nuit, le jour... Oh yes!

"She asked me to check out his studio. He's not there, but his car is."

"What the hell are you talking about?" Billy shouts, spilling ash on the rug.

Cher-cher l'ami... I'll find him for sure, my lover, I can feel it. I know it.

"She was worried sick about an accident...his car had been giving him trouble."

Billy puffs. "Information must be accompanied by insight."

"What? What the hell are you talking about?" The lover in France would not say much. Partly because of the language problem, partly his quiet nature.

"Never mind. You wouldn't understand. I thought you were going downtown to book your charter."

"I am, love, I am," I say, surprising Billy with sweetness.

God, I know his every manipulative move. He wants me out so he can get ready for the track without a hassle. But I don't give a goddamn. Not now, now that I've my new lover to flee to. I can out-manipulate even Billy.

"I have to wait for Peggy, but I won't be long. I'm in a rush to settle the ticket."

"Peggy?" He sets his cigar down on the ashtray, frowning.

"Tim's sister! In Baltimore! She phoned me all the way from Baltimore because she trusts me."

"Oh."

Jusque l'oublier... I'll forget all right. I'll forget Toronto, Billy, *Here*, and the bloody beginners art class.

"Coffee's made. Want some?"

Chan-ter l'amour... I sigh. Life drawings.

He butts his cigar. "I suppose." He lumbers into the kitchen, barefoot, unshaven, pajama-clad. My lover will go about naked. Yes.

I rush into the kitchen, get down Billy's yellow-checked mug, the only one he uses. 'Left over from my bachelor days,' he likes to say, even after 25 years. I take milk from the fridge, pour his coffee, pass him the sugar, while thinking about myself and my Frenchman drinking *café au lait* out of those big bowls. Our eyes meeting...

Billy is settling down. He's always better after coffee. I turn the oven to 350 degrees and put in the croissants. *Croissants. We'll feed them to each other, my French or Spanish lover and me.* Billy lunges over, turns the oven to 300. "I like them warmed, girl, not dried out." That's right. Try to make me feel guilty. Not any more, Billy. If I'm going to feel guilty, I'll bloody well do something to make it worthwhile. Really worthwhile.

He thought he had the house to himself for Nana, cigars, and racing statistics. I used to allow him this pasha role because I actually felt guilty about earning nothing painting; felt obliged to wait on him. But when I get back, after my big show, the reviews and all, I would not give a damn. Not a damn.

When the telephone rings, I grab it. Peggy. Even Peggy is an intrusion now. I've more important things on my mind. "Hello?"

"What did you find out, Alice? Is he—"

"Good news. Tim wasn't in, but his car is there, so you can stop worrying about an accident."

"Thank God...did you knock loud enough to rouse him?"

"I banged. I yelled, left a note, rapped on the window."

"Then he must be sick. He must be lying there with something... a depression... he gets depressed... I know. I'm a nurse."

"He didn't seem depressed when I saw him, Peggy. In fact, he was unusually cheery."

"Oh dear God! That's worse. Depressives hide it...a bad sign, cheeriness. Usually before a suicide attempt. Do you know those other friends of his? Kevin and Deirdre? Don't they live close? Find out if they know something before you call the police."

"You're that worried? Well okay. They do see each other all the time. Maybe there was a party and he stayed over. I'll phone them."

"Do that. I'll never forgive myself if he's lying sick in his room. Something's very wrong here...he'd have phoned to cancel. And he would not have cancelled this special weekend...disappointed his very own mother and Kathleen, at this very important family event. This is a crisis."

"If he promised, and the car is there, he's taken a bus. Maybe he even flew."

"With all the terrorists? Dear God! I hope not."

"I'll get Deirdre."

"Bless you, Alice. Please God, I hope he's not flying...I don't know what I'd do if Michael hadn't given me your number. I need someone reliable up there, Tim being the way he is. As I said before, I felt I knew you from all he told me. I'll call you back in an hour."

"Right." I hang up. What could Tim have told her about me? We meet on street corners; exchange keys through mail slots; leave notes under doors. Did I ever leave anything behind? Does Tim go through the waste-baskets? Would he do a sneaky thing like that? I hope not, because I was thinking that maybe my Frenchman or Spaniard could send his letters to Tim's. Another wave of cigar smoke hits me. Billy is blowing it my way deliberately. I do not react. Ha!

I dial Deirdre.

"Hello?"

"Hi. This is Alice O'Connell. I'm sorry to bother you Saturday morning, but Tim's sister phoned me from Baltimore."

"Why you? Like, she has our number. I gave it to her, when I, like, phoned Tim down there, once. That's weird."

"Michael gave her my number. For emergencies because I live right around the corner."

"We're just up the street!"

"Mike knows I'm an early bird. The thing is, Tim was supposed to arrive in Baltimore last night—"

"He was? I saw him at the co-op last night. He never told me. Like, we even invited him over, but he wouldn't come. Said he had to work—running off prints down at the college studio."

"That's it! He must have worked right through. Did he seem okay, Deirdre? His sister was worried that he's depressed."

"Depressed? Of course! So that's it! He has not been himself. Definitely. I'm so glad you told me, Alice. Like, it explains everything. He's been very quiet. Hardly speaks to me anymore. As if he's afraid of his feelings. For me. Oh my God. Alice, you forget about it and leave it all to me. I'll go right down."

"I already did. Just got back. He wasn't in, but his car was there."

"He wasn't there? Where did he spend the night? He's depressed! Severely depressed. Like, he's been so unfriendly... Retaliation, probably. Depression... he could be lying in there all alone."

What is she talking about? She thinks it's serious, too. "Oh my God!" I say. "Now I wish I'd kept his extra set of keys."

"You had keys to his studio? What for?"

"To work there. When he was gone. But I gave them to Maureen."

There's a silence. I hear a sharp intake of breath.

"Maureen! Why Maureen? How long has Maureen had his keys?"

"About a year. I'll try the studio once more. I left a note for him in case he was asleep. Maybe he's read it by now and will answer. When I go back."

"Don't count on it. Bad enough having no phone, but like, he won't even answer the door unless he feels like it. I've gone there time and time again. Knocked. Left notes. Now I know for sure that Maureen, like, intercepted them."

Ah no, Deirdre. I collected them with Tim's mail. *Wanta go to the Revue tonight? Howsabout coming up for Mexican food, amigo? Meecha at Livie's show tonight.* I wasn't being sneaky or anything. Just couldn't help it. Just written on sheets of paper. A-hah. I knew she had the hots for him!

"Kevin and I are *both so fond of Tim*. But he pulls away...
withdraws. A depression, that's it! If you can't rouse him, get
the superintendent to open the door. Find out if he's really in
there. Phone me as soon as you find out anything. If he's not
there we'll like, have to call the police."

"Goodbye, Deirdre."

Withdrawn. Was I fooled by his cheerful outburst?
Deirdre saw him last night. 'There's lots wrong with Tim.'
That from his sister, a nurse. What did I know? If he's killed
himself, the Frenchman, or the Spaniard, will help me forget.

Billy extends his mug. I reach for the coffee carafe and fill
it for him. Habit. Just habit.

"I was thinking about the new ignorance," he says. "Data
overload. So overwhelming and confusing—"

"That was Deirdre."

"Deirdre?"

"Up the street. Married to Kevin? The photographer."

"...that a person can't form a valid conclusion... "

"She saw Tim last night...said he was moody...wouldn't
speak to her."

"Who?"

"Deirdre."

"That figures."

"She thinks he's depressed too. Deirdre and Peggy both."

"Tim? Don't be crazy. He just wants peace and quiet. Like
me."

So do I. And love. Passion. Fame.

"I'll phone Mike and Maureen. See what they know."

"Keep out of this."

"I can't now." I dial, and hear, 'Hello. This is Michael
McKernan. I'm sorry about using this goddam machine, but
please leave a short message after the beep. We really want to
get back to you.' Wait. Beep.

"This is Alice. I've tried Tim's place. He's not in. His car is there. His sister and Deirdre think there might be something wrong. If you've seen him recently, call me immediately."

I hang up, open the oven door, grab tongs, lift out the croissants and dump them on Billy's plate. He squeezes them. They are just right. I know, because I've got the timing perfect by now, even when he changes the oven. I suppress a smile. If they weren't just right, he'd have an excuse to dump on me. Now I'm one up.

I head for the door. The bloody telephone rings again.

"The phone's ringing." Billy's mouth is full. He spreads plum jam on the other half of a croissant. My lover will be a delicate eater, a nibbler, take tiny bites with his perfect white teeth.

I run back. "It could be urgent." Billy takes another bite.

"Hello?"

"Hi there, Alice."

"Oh my God...it's you! Tim. You're alive!"

"Yes."

"Where are you?"

"I got up early and went out for coffee and donuts. When I got back I found your note, so I ran out to the phone booth. I've phoned my sister. Sorry you had to go through this. She gets like that."

"But she said you always phone."

"We had an unspoken agreement. I always phone just before I leave. She should know if I didn't phone it meant I wasn't leaving. She must have that figured out by now."

"She thought you'd been killed. She was going to call the police. What about your mother? And Kathleen's graduation?"

"I'm going later. I've work to do this weekend."

"You better phone Deirdre."

"Why Deirdre?"

"Because she thought you were like, depressed. So did Peggy... She asked me to check with all your friends. I've been running around all morning trying to track you down for Peggy."

"Thanks for your concern. I'll call Kevin and Deirdre."

"And Michael and Maureen. I left a message for them, after Deirdre told me about your depression. They're probably concerned too."

"Peggy. Kevin and Deirdre. Michael and Maureen. Jesus, anyone you missed, Alice?"

"That's about it."

"Thanks. Guess my day is shot making phone calls."

"I'm sorry, Tim. But I'm glad everything worked out...that you're okay. Goodbye." I slump against the telephone stand.

"Billy, my day is ruined." I say this, because I always say it. It's expected, but now I'm happy. There's France, the lover, the paintings, the reviews.

"It's your own fault, girl. I heard it all. The usual. Getting caught up in other people's problems. Get yourself a life. Those people you were talking to this morning were all Irish. My own people. I know them. Always fearing death and destruction. Right-brained. But that's why I've this gift for statistics. There's a handicapping expert called Kelly. Most racing experts are Irish."

"What's that got to do with Tim? I'll phone Margaret. I might as well cancel the chateau." I'm bluffing. Not in a million years. Never. Not with the lover and all waiting for me. I'll get myself a life, all right. And no way will he be bloody Irish. A Frenchman or a Spaniard. No wonder they so easily invaded Ireland. Why, the Irish met them with open arms. So will I.

"No way. Your behaviour this morning proves you need to distance yourself from people. Look how you got all caught up in everything. Over-involved. You're getting worse, as you age. Nagging me when I'm only trying to provide you with a better life. Your behaviour could be the onset of senility. A trip abroad will be just the ticket."

It would indeed, I thought, but continued with the game I was beginning to enjoy.

"But what if I don't like it in France? I'll have nobody to talk to," I say, smiling in my mind, knowing I'll not be talking.

"That'll do you á world of good. Yes. Not knowing the language will pull you back into yourself. Get you centred."

Centred, yes, flat on my back on a bed, under the Frenchman. Or the Spaniard.

"But I'll go crazy!"

"That's definitely possible. If you panic, just take the Cherbourg ferry from France over to Ireland. It goes straight across to Rosslare in Wexford. If you're cracking up, my family will see to you."

"Oh, I don't think—"

"You never think. You've got to learn how to shut out input. If you don't, you're ready for a breakdown."

"A breakdown?"

"A nervous breakdown. I see a vacation for you as preventive maintenance."

"A nervous breakdown?"

"If you don't shut off input and learn to be selective."

"You're right," I say, "I'll be selective." Thinking yes, I'll shop around. Be choosy. He'll be dark, intense, not too tall. Maybe a nice poet. Jealous. I grab my purse, open the door, run out and hear Billy yelling.

"Alice! Another coffee!"

I slam the door. Nana's song echoes in my head. *L'amour.* I smile. France, of course. *L'amour.* I skip down the front steps, singing.

Billy bellows inside.

green and gold

For Don Coles

 EAT assaults Jane as she nears the plane's exit and looks out at palm trees. She missed her med school graduation ceremony to visit her parents in Brazil; had struggled over her decision to come here; had resisted her need for ritual and recognition.

Graduation was a farce anyway. Middle class sham, her husband David says.

"Thank you for flying Varig. Have a good day." The stewardess smiles her perfect smile, opens wide her green-lidded eyes.

"Thank you." Jane and David pause, descend the stair-case, swept again by gusts of heat. They search for her parents among the small group on the tarmac.

Several months ago, back in Edmonton, her mother had phoned her crying. 'I don't want to go to Brazil. I'm too old to pull up roots. I'll feel trapped. And Dr Jacobson said the climate would aggravate my arthritis.' Jane winced. Always 'my arthritis,' that prize possession. She listens for this in patients. 'My high-blood pressure,' and even, dear God, 'my cancer.' A clue. Prognosis poor. The patient has claimed the illness. Owns it.

After that phone call she took her mother out for lunch to talk. Jane learned, as she grew older, that her father's foreign contracts were often a geographic conclusion to an affair. Universities were small towns. Things got around. Jane heard. Her mother either never found out about these affairs, or more likely, never let on she knew about them in order to avoid having to make a painful decision.

'You don't have to stay down there, Mom. Just go with Dad for a visit and give it a try. Find out if you like it first.'

'I have to decide right away so the University can arrange for our accommodation. If I do go I'll have to decide what to do about the house, all our things…'

'You might get depressed, away from your own friends, away from us. Northeastern Brazil is a bad area, David says. The poverty …'

'Oh I know what *David* says. David knows everything.'

Oh dear, wrong thing, that quote. Try again. 'Mom, do me a favour. If you do go, bring enough money for a return flight. That way you won't feel trapped. You don't have to tell dad anything about it, but it will give you a sense of choice.'

'Oh … I'd hate to keep anything from your father. It would be like lying.'

Jane sighed. Her mother irritated her, even angered her, but her simple honesty touched her.

Jane was relieved to see a large withdrawal from her mother's account to which she had access, her mother's savings from teaching. Dad would cut a swath down there. Still too damned attractive, even at sixty with silver-white hair, blue eyes, ski-tanned face. And there was something so intense, so athletic and young about his way of moving.

Not much skiing on the equator. Maybe he'd stay home more.

Her mother's letters were too happy. Brazil was beautiful, beautiful. She wrote of enjoying the luxuries of a maid, afternoon naps, a country club. 'I get to meet nice Brazilians who invite me to their homes to learn English. I seem to fit in. And there's a dear Dutch boy who visits me. We talk about farming in Alberta. You'd love him. Of course the Brazilians took to your dad right away. You should just hear him speak Portuguese.' Jane worried, thought, yeah, he's fitting in all right. Poor mom.

When her mother sent her a return ticket for a graduation gift, Jane knew she must visit. With David. But how could she persuade him? 'Mom's getting on,' she tried. 'And you know Dad. I've really got to go. Would you come with me, could we spare enough …?'

'Of course. That was great of Jessie, giving you a ticket. I'd love to go with you. We've got enough saved for me to come along.' His immediate consent surprised her. He wasn't that crazy about her mother. Or her father. Especially her father. Until he added, 'Lagoa Grande is near Recife. Dom Camaro country. Liberation theology. We'll be able to see what's going on for ourselves. We might even meet some real activists down there!'

'Right. Then it's settled.'

Now she sees her parents in the crowd, waving. Her mother, stuffed into a tight print dress is red-faced, perspiring. When Jane pushes ahead and reaches out to hug her, her mother bursts into tears. Her father, in loose Cuban guayaba and light slacks, is tanned, cool-looking. He shakes hands with David and asks, "How was the flight?"

"Impressive, Malcolm. Waiting at Belem airport was pure Graham Greene! It was so hot we could see steam rise from the jungle. I got a fantastic shot of the Amazon from the plane." David reaches out to hug her mother. "Hi there, Jessie."

"Graham Greene, eh?" her dad says. "We must go back that way, Jess. Rio might as well be Montreal."

Her mother moves out from David's hug, to reach for Jane's arms. "You look so nice. Professional." *So much for my new shirtmaker dress.*

"Janie, your hair's too short. Lady doctors!" Her father

says as he bends down to kiss her forehead. Jane shrugs her shoulders, and thinks, So what! David shakes his hand again and says, "Good to see you, Malcolm."

They all follow her father as he leads them through the crowd to a big white car with a huge red maple leaf logo on the side.

Pointing to it, her mother says, "Canadian government, Everyone respects us."

Jane and her mother clutch sweaty hands in the back seat; David and her dad chat up front. Jane sits up, suddenly keen, taking in the heat, sun shimmering on the road, thatched huts in the *sertao*, on the drive to Lagoa Grande. She smiles and squeezes her mother's hand at the sight of naked kids along the roadside. A little boy pees in the ditch.

"It's just like North Africa," David says.

There he goes, talking about his 60s travels, Jane thinks. To Europe, India. And smiles to herself. She stayed home and travelled—chemical trips—more interesting than David's, but not to be publicly discussed. Especially by a respectable doctor.

"Dave you're like all the other foreigners," her dad says. "They look at northeastern Brazil and compare it to Ontario, B.C., Texas. Right, Jess?"

Jane knows her father puts David down because he disapproves of him. And of her. "Why can't you get real jobs? All that money I spent on medical school. Now it's 'Native People' this and 'Aboriginal' that. When I was a boy they called them Indians. They're still Indians."

"It gets more like the foothills near Lagoa. It'll remind you of Alberta, Jane."

"See what I mean?" her father nudges David.

Although exhausted from the long hot flight, Jane is reviving as she stares eagerly out the window. Her eyes are bright, alert, at the sight of miles of sugar cane; women washing clothes in a pond; a naked little kid riding a burro; Brahma cattle grazing in miles of blue-green pasture; and palms, palms, palms, forming green tunnels over the road. It won't be too bad after all, she decides. She'd come here out of concern for her mother, but now she thinks it could be fun. She reaches out and puts her arm around her mother, gives her a hug. "This is exciting!" she exclaims.

Her mother beams. "I'm glad, dear. You deserve a change. You need it after working so hard. A doctor! Imagine that. I'm so proud. And it was nice that David could come, too."

Her father interrupts, "We're nearing our watering-hole. It's about midway and breaks the drive." He slows down the car as they reach a bus station.

He parks over on one side and leads them to an open restaurant. He strides ahead and claims a table, pushing his tall frame through a group of short dark Brazilians. Jane observes faces. Wonderful, beautiful faces. Mixed. African, Indian, Portuguese. *They* turn from the counter to stare at *them*, grinning. Jane and David smile back. "Friendly people," David says.

"*Cuatros Antarcticas,*" her father commands.

Jane smirks, watching. *Imperious. Presence—he's got it. Could claim the earth was flat and have a following. Of women.* A waiter scurries to their table, sets down bottles and glasses.

"Look, Jane." David peels the label from the beer bottle. "See the trademark? A penguin. Antartica. We're closer to it down here." David smiles, says, "Yeah," and carefully peels the label from his damp bottle.

"Another for your wonderful international collection," Jane comments. David's smile vanishes. He frowns, flattens the label on the plastic table top.

"Brahma Chopp is the other beer," her dad says. "Chopp means draft. It's a light pilsener. Myself, I've gone native—

for me it's *cachaca*—a rough cane liquor the locals drink. Knock-out. We'll have *batidas* at our party next week. That's *cachaca* and passion-fruit juice. Did your mother tell you about our party, Jane?"

"No.... I didn't know it was on for sure..." Jessie says, "how they'd feel."

"It's on, Jessie," her dad announces. Jane wants to hit him.

"Did you bring a long dress, dear?"

"One of my Indian prints, yes."

"Oh, no! Not one of those old hippie things? I meant a *nice* dress."

"I love it. It's cotton. Cool. Great for this climate. Besides, I didn't expect anything formal."

"Our handbook advised us to bring long dresses. For evening parties. I've had Lucia, a dressmaker here, run some up."

"How colonial. Like the good old days. The British in India." Her mother's face falls. Jane wishes she hadn't said that.

LAGOA GRANDE. Jane is less upset than David and the other constantly-complaining Canadians about people spitting on sidewalks; by beggars, drunks, sick people. Better get used to it, David, she thinks, watching him head for the shower as soon as he gets in. There are no showers up north where we're going.

They pass the days reading, sleeping in late, or visiting craft markets; and at her mother's insistence, making afternoon visits to the Clube Campestre. Jane observes that her mother has cultivated a tan that makes her look like a big leather purse. She wears a bright fuchsia bathing suit with a skirt around it, the kind fat women wear.

Jane enjoys the pool, the sun. In her sensible one-piece blue suit she envies the Brazilian women, not just their

bikinis, but their way of moving proudly, naturally, regard-
less of weight or age. *Maybe a yellow string bikini?*
    Jane worries. Her mother only enters the water to cool off
from sunbathing or between drinks. And she is drinking too
much.
    "You should swim lengths, Mom. A little exercise will
help your joints."
    "I'm not so sure, dear. I just listen to my body." A familiar
line. Jane's sister Beverly's. A vegetarian, her life committed
to skiing; working off-and-on as a waitress in Banff. Her
dad's favourite. He sends money to support her go-with-the-
body lifestyle, but refuses to send anything to Jane to set up
her practice.
    Her mother prepares for the party, and is nervously
phoning around to invite people. The Mannings, the Clarks,
the Gagnons from Quebec. 'You can practise your French,
David!' She drags Jane to the hairdresser's, and to her
surprise, Jane has fun. They giggle together, getting
manicures and pedicures, picking out nail-polish colours.
    Jane is surprised, also, at her mother's apparent
proficiency in Portuguese. She chats with the manicurist, the
hairdressers, and they respond. She'll be okay here after all,
Jane decides. Her mom can take charge, hold her own
without Dad.
    Jane still dreads the party and is relieved when the day
arrives. Geralda has been making various kinds of snacks,
spearing cubes of cheese with toothpicks. Jane decides to
bake her favourite, her hippie '60s carrot cake. Minus the
mood-altering herbs. Geralda is entranced, and Jane, from
David's Portuguese dictionary, announces, *'um bolo do
cenoura,'* as she slathers the top with cream-cheese icing.
Geralda gets the giggles. The idea of carrots and cheese, in a
cake, is so strange to her.
    But the evening, aside from Jane's triumph with the cake,

is an ordeal. The guests are five Canadian couples, several young Brazilians, and Manuela, her father's assistant, a small dark beauty in a strapless white dress with a bare panel exposing her flat brown belly. Manuela passes drinks and canapés as if she were the hostess, while Jane's mother knocks back gin-and-tonic. Three Brazilian girls question Jane in careful English. They are accompanying their husbands to Canada on exchange programmes and assume automatic acceptance into med schools. *Lots of luck.*

The party would have been an agony, a total bore, without Hans, the Dutch agronomist, her mother's young friend. He's warm and friendly and seems really fond of her mom. Hans is dark, stocky, and is fluent in English. Jane likes him herself, and is pleased to see how well he and David are hitting it off. He invites them to visit the mountain *cooperativo* where he works with Redemptorist priests, and to a hospital there improvised by a Belgian doctor-priest who takes care of the poor and trains his own medical assistants. Jane is eager to meet him. And relieved. David was getting edgy, irritable with her mother's plans. He was disappointed not to find out more about what was going on politically in this region of Brazil. And she herself is excited about the invitation from Hans. She might really learn something.

Jane keeps smiling, nodding, circulating; avoiding Manuela, who keeps trying to get chummy. When Manuela starts talking about the lab work, Jane even deliberately yawns. But Manuela goes on and on, her smile and talk perpetual. It is early in the morning by the time the guests straggle out.

Her mother hugs Jane. "It was such a success! Everyone loved you. There will probably be more parties now, for you and David. Brazilians are like that."

"No, Mom, I'm not up for any more parties."

Her mother smiles. "We'll see."

Her father and David happily sip a nightcap of Chivas Regal.

"Hans is great," David says. "Those priests sound interesting."

"They're interesting all right. Under police surveillance. Nothing but troublemakers. We're not visiting any goddamn priests."

"Malcolm's right, David. That's just what Dona Marcia, my English pupil, says. We really shouldn't ... "

"We're going," Jane declares.

"Not with me. Not in our car." her father announces. "I've a job to consider. Somebody in this family has to earn a living."

Tell that to Beverly.

"I'm considering *my* job," Jane asserts, turning to confront her dad. "This doctor-priest can probably give me better ideas for my practice up North than I'll ever learn interning in Edmonton hospitals." She traces her finger around the wild print of her Indian skirt, smells patchouli. Its scent still clings, despite the years, and Geralda's loving handwashing. *Vancouver. Making candles that summer. 1971? My first time in the ocean. Mountains. I'll leave the dress for Geralda.*

"Well, I'm *not* going," her father announces, "and you're *not* taking our car."

"But Malcolm," her mother says, "it should be all right. The Canadian *presence* among the poor. Showing that we care."

"I don't want that car seen out there," he commands. Her mother pleads and frets. Next day Hans averts a crisis when he phones to offer a jeep more suited to the rough terrain.

* * *

JESSIE is relieved when Zé, the driver, stops the jeep. Thank God. The little Brazilian was either deliberately scaring her or else he just enjoyed being in the driver's seat. The jeep saved the day, thanks to dear Hans. He is like a son, dropping in Sundays when Geralda is off, and Malcolm is out working at the University. 'It's so damned hard translating everything, Jess,' Malcolm explained. Sundays would be awful without Hans.

Hans helps her out, shakes hands with Zé. "*O mismo como* Fittipaldi," he comments. They all laugh. Jessie smooths her sticky cotton skirt, stretches her aching knees, and rubs the pain in her back. She looks around to see piles of bricks near a church, several small new homes, and more bricks stacked near half-finished walls. A tall, lean man strides from the church to greet them. Jessie observes his plaid shirt, jeans, cropped grey hair; his bright blue eyes behind steel-rimmed glasses. She is immediately taken with him. He looks just like Gary Cooper, she thinks, except for the hair and glasses. The priest nods to them, speaks quickly to Hans in Dutch, frowning. He waves and hurries off.

"He apologized for leaving," Hans explains. "He has to go to Recife. Two priests there have been jailed, so he's gone to try and get them out. They were begging bread from rich people and distributing it in the street to petty thieves and whores at outdoor Masses. Someone in Brasilia calls this communism."

Jessie is disappointed that the good-looking priest has gone. Such a kind face. But she is confused. Brasilia is a nice *clean* city. The nicest place she had visited in Brazil. It's the capital, so people there must know what they are doing.

She is pleased, though, to follow Hans and David, to have Jane beside her, and to leave Zé, that crazy little driver. Like a child with a toy, behind the wheel. So tiny, like most people in the Northeast. No wonder people adore Malcolm. His height.

They reach a rambling, one-storey building surrounded by coconut palms, guava, papaya and avocado trees. Jessie can identify them all because when she can't sleep at night, she reads. She reads up on tropical fruits, plants, flowers. A leftover *fazenda*, she decides. Hans rings the bell.

Jessie pushes aside a branch of flaming jacarandas, and when she hears hummingbirds, she nudges David.

"The Portuguese word for hummingbird is *besaflor*, David. That means 'flower-kisser.' Isn't that cute?"

"Nice," he acknowledges, and although he smiles thoughtfully for a moment, he ignores her comment and resumes talking to Hans. Some linguist, Jessie thinks.

She turns to her daughter and whispers, "You know, Jane, if I were really ill, I'd have no hesitation about coming out here to see this Dr Ahermaa. The priest-doctor? Or whatever. Even Dona Marcia, my English pupil, said so. Her husband is a doctor, and he and the other doctors consult him all the time. On the q.t. All he asks for in return are antibiotic samples, but Brazilian specialists expect the skies. He'll even settle for a bottle of cognac. He's a drinker. I wish you had let me bring that bottle of cognac as a friendly gesture. Here they call it 'cognac-i.' Got to put a *vowel* on the end of everything."

Jane sets her lips. Jessie doesn't like this, knows it means her daughter is angry, is holding something back. About what, she wonders. My mentioning the cognac? She keeps at me about drinking. But she's always been so moody. Always. She looks so young with her hair cut short. It still curls tightly in the heat. Like when she was little. Couldn't get a brush through it. She reaches out to touch Jane's hair and says, "Dona Marcia actually speaks English very well. She studied for years at the Language Institute, with Americans. But she wanted to practise with me because she thinks that Canadian accents are nicer. I'm flattered. It's a real break, socially. Dona Marcia knows everything and everybody in Lagoa Grande."

Jessie feels weepy because Jane not only does not respond, she isn't even listening. Here she is, trying to get close to Jane, and she's being ignored. She's hurt because of David's indifference, because the nice-looking priest left, because Malcolm is angry, and because the heat always makes her feel weepy. So do Brazilians.

Dona Marcia and that transaction last week. Twenty-five cruzeiros to the dollar. Bobby Jean from the American mission got thirty in Recife at the black market, at that seedy Spanish hotel. The Basque.

All Dona Marcia had really wanted from me, she realizes, was dollars.

And I thought she was my only friend, besides Hans. Canada? Go back? Husbands not safe in the Northeast. Patricia, the coordinator, had warned her, eight women to each man. Aggressive Brazilian women. Whispers of broken marriages; wives whisked home; husbands' contracts extended.

Malcolm laughed when he told her the first questions put to him by his assistant, Manuela. 'Are you married?' 'Did your wife accompany you?'

Finally, 'Does she like it here?'

And chuckling. 'These girls are so desperate they'll settle for any arrangement.'

He said I should go back with Jane for a visit to escape the rainy season.

No, dammit. I'll stay. Arthritis or no arthritis.

* * *

Zé dusts the seats, the dashboard. Car. Driving. Power. Beside Hans. Going to town with Hans. Buying faucets, hose. Beer with Hans in Lagoa. Like a friend. What's the catch? Zé offered names, introductions. Hans says no, his own girl is coming from Holland. Like priests? No, Hans, just different. Lives with us, not with the *tecnicos* in Gringo Palace.

Zé lights a cigarette from a pack given to him by Father van Geffen. Those *Redemptoristas,* what guys. First the brick *cooperativo.* Our own houses. Better than before, in huts made of cartons, at the edge of the da Costa's, depending on leftover food sneaked out by maids. Soon beans from the rigged-up irrigation Hans helped them build.

Zé smiles and gives the back seat a swipe with the cloth. The da Costa family put up big signs forbidding people to pick fruit. A joke. Most people can't read. Who needs to? In Lagoa, things get around. Father van Geffen visited the da Costas, asked for oranges that would go to waste. They gave him a big basketful. That day. Then they joined the big new church, the other one. Run by Americans. Gave them money for special electric guitars and fancy coloured lights.

Religion. What is it? Priests? They work with us, make bricks. Fix the land, grow beans, dry them. Dig a pond for fish. Houses, beans, fish.

These Canadian kids. Pretty little girl, but too serious. Her husband short, dark, like a *Brasileiro.* Hans tried to explain what he does. Helps the Indians get back their land. They have lost their land? Zé thought there were Eskimos in Canada. He is proud of his own Indian blood. His father's name, Moacir, was Indian.

Dona Jessie. Poor old fat lady. Zé flicks the rag across the hood. Nothing wrong with being fat. He likes his women fat. Young ones. It's the way she looks all fenced in, bulging over tight dresses. She wanted to bring the fancy white car with the red leaf on the door. People thought it belonged to a big-shot tobacco salesman. But the leaf is from some tree that grows in Canada.

Crazy. Zé chuckles, spits on the cloth, polishes door handles. Professor Malcolm parks his car right in front of Manuela's every Sunday afternoon. Lucky guy, laying

Manuela. She is beautiful, a jewel. Professor Malcolm fits in all right. A *bem Brasileiro*.

Speeding around corners high in the Barbaremas, Zé had smiled. The terror in Dona Jessie's eyes, her grey hair flying.

* * *

JESSIE wipes the sweat from her face with a fresh linen handkerchief. Hans knocks on the hospital door. Soon a short, tired-looking man in his sixties comes to greet them. He is white-haired, balding; cheeks grizzled as though he hadn't shaved. He wears his shirt loose over dark pants. What kind of a doctor is this? Jessie wonders. He embraces Hans but remains unsmiling during introductions. A stern man.

Chatter. About the language of operation? Yes. David understands a bit of everything. When he interrupts in French, Dr Ahermaa's face brightens. He looks at David and obviously approves of him right away. Why? Because of his French? His enthusiasm? His beard? The beard. Like Ché Guevara. Radicals always recognize each other. Like homosexuals.

Speaking French, David seems like a new person, is less earnest, his face and gestures become animated. He looks just like them—the French in Quebec. Malcolm took her to Montreal on their honeymoon, and it was her first trip away from Alberta. She'd been homesick the whole time. But even then, Malcolm fit in. Even spoke French. She felt left out from the very start.

Why do people change speaking a foreign language? Malcolm becomes a stranger speaking Portuguese at parties. He smiles a lot, touches people, waves his arms. Speaking English, he is more dignified and controlled. Her husband. Hers.

David breaks into English. "The police raided last week. They do this once a month, but they don't like to because they're all Catholic. The last time they raided during some kind of fever. Two babies had just died. The families were crying."

Jessie stiffens. She'd glimpsed a row of coffins in the storage room off the corridor. *The worst thing about Brazil. Coffins everywhere. At home, thank God, they're out of sight.*

David and the doctor are so involved in French discussion that David forgets to interpret until he has some real gem. Then his face lights up, he blurts. "He says he came here from the Belgian Congo!"

Jane fidgets, interrupts. "I want to see his set-up. Could we get on with it?" David translates. The doctor walks ahead, beckons them to follow. At the end of a long corridor a black, short-haired dog sleeps near a window. Not really a window, just an opening in the wall. Sun beats in on the dog's back. The animal twitches; disturbed by flies.

There are small wards off the corridor with three steel cots to a wall; and in the centre, a table holds coconuts with straws in them. Another dog, a brown one, sleeps beside a patient's bed. Jessie watches the doctor speak to his patients, gently touch them through bleach-worn sheets.

"Ask him about the dogs, David. And find out what's in the coconuts." *That drink in Acapulco. Coco loco? Or something. Tequila. Rum. Our twenty-fifth anniversary. Malcolm's surprise. I got that terrible sunburn and had to stay inside. The whole time.*

"Patients are allowed to bring their pets," David says in English, after a brief discussion with Ahermaa. "Sometimes their pets are all they have. And that's just coconut water in the coconuts. It's safe, free, grows on the grounds. It contains nutrients. Besides, they believe in it and they can't afford bottled water."

"Oh." She nudges Jane. "Dogs! Isn't that unsanitary?"

"I like it," Jane says. "I think it's a good idea."

Fancy medical schools. Foothills Hospital as bad as those back East. Meet the patient's emotional needs and never mind the rabies. Or parasites. Dogs carry them, and their fleas carry leishmaniasis, a tropical illness. Jessie read all this in her medical encyclopaedia, boning up on tropical diseases.

"Look, Mom, the lab." Her daughter's face finally brightens. It is a tiny white room the size of her powder-room back home. There are steel tables, shelves, microscopes, test tubes. Jars.

"It's perfect!" Jane enthuses. "Exactly what I want." Dr Ahermaa smiles and puts his arm around her. Priests and doctors get off on Jane, Jessie observes. Her work, her heroic work and dedication. Her bright, child's eyes. David has probably told them they will live on a reserve without light or water. Jessie knows Jane is smiling because of Ahermaa's approval, that she needs it, laps it up.

It wasn't Malcolm's fault he and Jane didn't get along. He had to work hard and was away so much. Jane never really tried to please him. She had always been too serious. Then taking off for Vancouver and going wild on drugs. And marrying an Easterner, moving up North. Perhaps if she'd been athletic like Beverly ... Jessie frowns, swats a fly.

David and Ahermaa continue in French, which Jane apparently understands, because she nods, asks questions. When did she learn this? Occasionally David interrupts and translates for her. The priest says something and they laugh. Jessie fights tears. Everyone speaking French, understanding each other. That feeling ... her honeymoon.

"What's going on?" Jessie asks.

Jane points to three jars of brown stuff. David chuckles and explains, "Dr Ahermaa calls it expensive shit. Rich people's from Lagoa Grande. Because he is an expert on intestinal parasites, they consult him instead of their own doctors."

What kind of priests talk like that? Jessie frowns, and winces when she notices his nicotine-stained fingers shaking. A-ha! She too, needs a drink.

They follow Ahermaa out of the lab around a corner to a dingy kitchen. It is cool, on the building's shady side.

"My liv-ing-room," Ahermaa sounds out carefully in English, smiling at Jessie.

Obviously. Jessie notices rows of empty cognac bottles under the sink. Ahermaa waves towards several rickety chairs.

They all sit down while Dr Ahermaa speaks to Hans, who explains, "He told me to go into the residence and bring back the new Dutch volunteer—a nurse who arrived last week. We'll be right back."

Ahermaa opens a cupboard and takes out a bottle of cognac.

A little brown bird flies in through an opening, perches on a shelf and chirps. Jessie looks around. There are other birds in a wicker cage. And at the far end of the room in a metal cage is an enormous parrot, a green and gold macaw. Her encyclopaedia describes them as 'gregarious but monogamous.' Precious because it is an endangered species, and because of its colours, the colours of Brazil. Jessie was so excited about that because green and gold were also the colours of Alberta.

Ahermaa watches Jessie watch the parrot.

"Romeo," he says. As if recognizing its name, the parrot Romeo preens for her, flaunts his colours. He pauses on his perch and trains his bright beady eyes on her. She stares right back, smiling; reminded of the Rio carnival, of the flamboyant men. Also of her medical encyclopaedia. *Psittacosis.* That deadly disease carried by parrots.

She shifts her bulky body on the small wooden chair to ease her joints. This is no country for girdles. What is Mal-

colm doing, home alone? Will he make sure the *empregada*
doesn't wreck tonight's roast chicken with cumin? She
wishes Ahermaa would hurry with the cognac, watching
desperately as he rips plastic, pulls the cork.

Hans returns to introduce Anna, a big Dutch girl. She
smiles as she circles the group and shakes hands vigorously
with everyone, then awkwardly rushes to help Ahermaa
with the glasses.

He brings a tumbler half-full to Jessie. She looks at her
watch, at Jane. It's not even noon. It would be rude to refuse.
Jane smirks. Ahermaa puts the glass firmly in Jessie's hand,
looks her squarely in the eye and smiles. He clinks his
tumbler against hers.

Anna passes drinks to the others. Smaller ones. She sits
down and spreads her knees out, leans over and stretches her
big arms across the wide stiff skirt. She has freckles and frizzy
auburn hair. Jessie decides she had been a farm girl before she
became a nurse.

They chat in English, French, Portuguese, Dutch. The
wild bird flies over to perch near the caged ones.

Ahermaa smiles at Jessie, then tops her drink, and his
own.

The black dog wanders into the cool kitchen and plunks
down at Jessie's feet, leaning against her leg. His weight, the
physical contact, is comforting to her. So is the cognac.

The young people smile, observing the wild bird and the
caged ones checking each other out. Jessie and Ahermaa
exchange glances. Jessie thinks, Why, he's like an old friend.
It's as though we've always known each other.

Together, they watch the parrot. She wishes now she had
learned French, so she could really talk to Ahermaa. She
wants to tell him that she wonders how the parrot feels, that
she wonders what it would feel like to be so extravagantly
beautiful.

wild cotton

MOLLY watches Patrick lead her into the art gallery for Beth's opening. Now he hands Molly the programme, trying to interest her. Well, she thinks, he can't, because I'm up here watching. That's just my body down there, and it's only there because Patrick dragged it. She likes watching him drag her body around. Downtown, uptown, to movies, and out to dinner. Out to dinner always, because the body lies in bed and refuses to cook. Just picks at food. Patrick persists. He is determined, he says, to pull her out of it.

Out of her grief over Phoebe's death. When did she die? A month ago? Two months? Yes, August... Phoebe's brother telephoned. Molly dropped the receiver and shivered. When Patrick came home Molly was outside her body; up here, looking down, watching him pour brandy into her mouth; cover her body with blankets. The brandy spilled because her teeth were chattering.

Phoebe. Giggling with her about guys at the Banff Fine Arts Centre. Yes, that's where we met. Two crazy teen-agers. Phoebe, from Vancouver. So sophisticated, I'd thought. Me, the up-country bumpkin. Keeping in touch all those years. 'Like sisters.' People said that about us—about Phoebe and me.

Beth was an artist friend of Phoebe's. Not my friend, no. Phoebe's, from art college. I was a bit jealous then, back at university, at how friendly Beth and Phoebe became. But I was busy with all the action at university, with making new friends.

Then I met Patrick and fell in love. After we married and moved to Toronto, Phoebe followed to teach art, and she became part of our family, godmother to Patsy and Brian.

Molly only met Beth at openings, or at parties. But that day, the day of Phoebe's mastectomy, Beth held Molly's hand.

Now Beth keeps phoning to cheer her up. Talks of boyfriends, painting, clothes. Molly says 'hm-hm.' Wonders, does Beth call because she misses Phoebe and needs a new friend? When she invited Molly to her opening, Molly said, 'I can't promise, it depends. How I feel that day.'

Opening day. 'I'm too tired,' Molly complained.

'Get dressed,' Patrick said.

She watches the body slide into the rust wool dress Phoebe had given her. Hand woven, from Quebec. She wore it to the funeral. She saw Patrick frown, knows he thought, dear God, not again. Over the dress she threw a multi-coloured serape that Phoebe brought back from Mexico. Patrick hates it. 'People don't take you seriously in a serape,' he said. 'They think you're an aging hippie or a phoney artist.'

Today he asked, 'You're wearing that?'

'Phoebe gave it to me.'

He frowned.

'It's an art show,' she watches her mouth say. 'A poncho and serape crowd. Of course, if you'd rather we stayed home...'

'No. We're going.' He leapt ahead and opened the door. Dragged her body into the car, out of the car, into the gallery. Got a glass of white wine, placed it in the icy hand sticking out of the rust sleeve.

Beth leaves a group, rushes to embrace the serape. The rust arm holding the glass goes down stiffly. Click. Chatter. People. Clever comments. The body inside the rust dress follows the man. Its head tilts to one side before a painting. It has been here before; knows what to do. Says, "How innovative." Maybe someone down there thinks the robot in the serape is a crazy sculptor's idea of an art patron. Does it have a number? A name? Yes. Grief in the Gallery.

Beth looks at the man. Molly knows this look means, 'She'll get over it. She'll be all right.' Molly watches from above, thinks, 'Like hell I will.'

Wine oils the machine. The robot starts moving more smoothly. The man is a good mechanic, knows his machine.

Whoops! Down in the gallery. Into her body again. Beth and Patrick.

"Your new work is great," Molly lies, pausing before a painting of a weather-beaten barn. "I love the water-colours." She fingers Beth's shawl. "And you look gorgeous." Beth, like Phoebe, loves clothes and bright colours. Her pink shawl is handpainted; her dress is purple and silky. But Beth herself is hard-edged. She wears her black hair in a short geometric cut. It is really grey, but Molly knows she dyes it. Molly liked it better grey—the softness. But Beth changes her look the way other artists change their styles, changes herself instead of her paintings. Currently Beth cultivates a flapper look, her skirt short above long silken legs. Her water-colours, however, are about the same as they were twenty years ago. Barns, flowers, mountains. Her barns are famous. They sell.

Molly fingers Beth's shawl. "Nice," she lies again. Remembers, Phoebe loved texture. Tweed. Wool. She could knit Phoebe a sweater. A pebbly bouclé to keep her warm. No...

Whoops! Up here again. Watching. Remembering. Mother's plush-covered album, filled with pictures of great-grandparents, aunts, uncles. All in coffins. A good idea. Photographs make death real.

*   *   *

MOLLY walks along Queen Street in the sunshine to the picture-framer's with the water-colour Patrick dutifully bought from Beth. They always buy one. It will join others on what Patrick calls their 'barn wall.' Despite his reminders about framing, the painting stayed on her mother's pine hutch for weeks. Now Molly finally follows through. Patrick will be relieved.

This morning she even cleaned and defrosted the fridge and washed the bathroom floor and tiles. Like that man in the TV commercial, the one emerging from the whirlwind. Not the Man from Glad, somebody else. But it brought her down into her body again, all the cleaning and activity. And the bright sun made her feel warmer.

As she opens the picture-framer's door, an alarm sounds. Is she a robber?

An unsmiling man descends the staircase to the left side of the cluttered shop. Although he is dark, good-looking, and tall, Molly is turned off by his clothes. He wears a red neckerchief, T-shirt, shiny blue pants. As if he dressed up to look like his idea of an artist.

Molly enters and removes the water-colour from a large envelope, and hands it to him. "I need some framing done," she says.

"Of course."

He holds up the painting, smiles, and exclaims, "What a relief! Real painting. A Beth Adams barn! Not that crap." He waves at framed community college diplomas and nursing school graduation photographs. "You must pick out just the right accents to do this piece justice," he advises, reaching for frame samples and mattes. He passes these to her.

"You decide," she says, handing them back.

He plays around and selects a double matte: a thin rim of green, a pewter frame. He holds them against Beth's painting, awaiting Molly's approval.

"Okay," she says, and nods.

"Lovely," he says. Then, "You might be interested in my gallery." He beckons her to the staircase.

"Come," he says. He begins to mount the stairs and stands waiting on the second step.

She shrugs, hesitates, mumbles, "I really…"

"Come," he commands, so she follows him upstairs. He opens a door, sweeps his hand in a grand gesture, and announces, "My gallery."

The 'gallery' is a small bedsitting-room, its walls jammed with drawings, acrylics, photoetchings. Molly freezes at the sight of two black-and-white charcoal drawings on a wall across the room. Their black-and-whiteness dominates the colours. A leering skull, a coiled snake. She shivers.

"Mine," he boasts. "They are scary. I was just playing around with those."

She moves on to some rather pleasant water-colours and stops to read the artist's name. It's some Italian she never heard of.

"Trudeau has one of his," the man says. "So has Alberto Moravia."

There are some cyanotype seascapes by another unfamiliar artist and lots of oils. But Molly's mind is filled with the image of the skull, the snake. The picture-framer watches her stalling and realizes she is not interested in buying, so strides towards the door. "Back to business."

Downstairs again they discuss prices, a deposit.

"When will these be done?" Molly asks.

"Whenever you want. Tomorrow? Friday? Saturday?"

"That soon?"

"For you, of course. I want to make you happy. I will. You'll see."

"Saturday then." She hurries towards the door.

"Just a minute," he calls. "Your receipt."

"Oh... yes." She answers absently. Skull. Snake.

The picture-framer has a pen and a receipt book in his hand.

"Your name. Just your first name, please."

"Molly."

"Molly. Phone number?"

"657-7556."

She shouldn't have done that. Given him her number. That novel by Muriel Spark. Death phoning everybody. Every. Body.

He gives her the receipt and clasps her extended hand. She feels herself start to drift upwards. *No. Scary up there.* She must run. She leaves the door ajar and hears a phone ring as she flees. Phone ringing is bad. Phoebe's brother telephoned. Now the picture-framer has her number. She fights, tries to stay down inside herself again.

At home she slams the door and rushes to phone Beth to keep the line busy; to tell her about the crazy picture-framer; his skull and snake pictures. About her fear.

"Don't tell Patrick, please, Beth, it's just that everything seemed sinister. And I was starting to feel better."

"That man was sinister," Beth says. "But I think your fear comes from your own grief or he wouldn't scare you." There is a silence, and Beth asks, "What about the Writers' Retreat? I promised Phoebe I'd get you there. She worried about you losing touch. Have you heard anything yet?"

"I was accepted. But it was so hard even to write that one sample story. It's too late for me to start writing again. I've lost it. I only made the effort for Phoebe's sake. I don't really care..."

"You should care. For yourself. And Patrick. You should go for his sake. I don't know how he's stood your morbidity. You've got to do something yourself. Make an effort to work, dammit!" Molly sighs, and Beth says, "I'm sorry Molly. Molly?"

"You're right. I'll call you later, 'bye."

Molly's knuckles are white and she shivers, clutching the receiver. She hangs up, pours brandy and runs a hot tub. She undresses and sits in the hot water to absorb heat. Then she towel-dries her body briskly, working up more heat, wraps herself in Patrick's flannel robe.

Six months ago. A warm day. Early spring. Garden smells. Phoebe. The hospital. 'You look like hell, Molly, you're wasting too much time here. You were so active at university. The paper, the quarterly. You quit writing and became a faculty wife, a gallery groupie, a professional parent. Patrick never expected that. For God's sake make something of yourself! Here. I asked a friend for this. For you...' Phoebe flung the Writers' Retreat application at her. She'd been hurt by Phoebe's rage but felt she should at least try. She wrote a story at Phoebe's bedside and found it difficult after years of not writing. She set it in the past, the 50s, of course. University. A period piece that nobody would want to read now. But it was something to do while Phoebe dozed, passing in and out of sleep, occasionally reaching for Molly's hand.

She dresses. Hears the door opening. Patrick's home. Just in time.

She rushes downstairs to greet him. "I'm going away. Remember that writers' thing? In October, if that's okay."

"Really? Great! Let's drink to that." He drops his briefcase, throws his coat on the sofa, strides into the kitchen and takes a bottle of red from the rack. He opens it and finds glasses. He pours two and hands one to Molly.

"Cheers," he says. He smiles, loosens his tie and stretches his neck with relief.

"Cheers," Molly responds, and reaches out to touch his glass with hers.

* * *

OCTOBER. Molly is packing. She stops. "I can't leave you, Patrick. I'll be all alone. I won't know anyone there. It'll be awful. I'll miss you. Why this big push to ship me off to hell-and-gone in Northern Ontario?"

"You're not being 'shipped.' It's an opportunity." He grabs her suitcase and packs for her. She watches him frown at her tracksuits. He goes to the closet, takes out her maroon velvet pants, folds them carefully.

"I won't wear those," she says, "so don't bother."

He ignores her and packs them, then carries her bag and typewriter out to the car. "Come on, let's go." She dawdles behind him. He lets her in and buckles her seatbelt as if he expected her to escape.

She watches him drive, his blue eyes squinting at the road. She sees that he is tense, worried. Occasionally he reaches up and runs his long fingers through his grizzled hair. An old, familiar gesture that showed worry. He has put up with a lot, she thinks. I should try harder.

"The leaves are turning," she offers. "Northern Ontario is gorgeous in autumn."

He smiles. "You're talking! It's the scenery." He holds her hand for the rest of the drive and is still smiling a few hours later as he parks, lets her out, leads her into the lodge, and signs her in. She lurks at the entrance.

He rushes back to her. "Looks like an interesting group. I saw names on the guest list. Big names. Come in Molly, let's explore." He leads her to a lounge with a huge fireplace; then out to a pool, to the bar.

"This is great, sweetie," he says. "I wish I could stay." He carries her bag and typewriter to her room, stands by the window and pulls the drapes apart.

"Look at the lake, Molly. What a view!" When she doesn't budge, he inspects her bed, bureau, and finally sets her typewriter on the desk.

"You're in business now, kid." When he kisses her, she clings, nuzzles, tries to change his mind. But he catches on and pulls away.

"You must stay. You need new people. Phoebe worried about that. She said you'd become her shadow."

"Her shadow?" Molly reaches out and hugs him, tries to cling again.

"No. Don't pull that..." he smiles. He grabs her shoulders. "Hey, just a minute, Molly. Surprises." He rushes away, outside to the car, and returns with a parcel. He hands it to her, brushes her cheek with a light kiss and darts quickly out the door. She drops the parcel, tries to follow, but he has vanished around a corner and shut the door.

She turns and plunks down on the bed. She unwraps the parcel, and fingers a soft cashmere sweater in deep burgundy from Beth; a batik silk scarf in hues of pale pink through to burgundy. Phoebe colours. Look good on Phoebe.

Her son Brian had advised her to bring tracksuits and sports clothes. 'It's a lodge, Ma. That's what people wear. You need to keep up your morning runs. Exercise is the best anti-depressant.'

It keeps me down on the ground, she thinks. She tosses the scarf and sweater into the bottom bureau drawer, sits on the bed and stares out at the lake. It's dusk. Bleak. The birches are cold and white. She hates this time of year, this time of day. This time of life.

What time? She looks at her watch. Five. It'll be safe to head for the bar. She's cold despite the over-heated room, so pulls on her heavy ski sweater and pants, her thick socks.

In the bar two groups of fashionably-clad women are holding court. Has she stumbled into a Vogue ad? Strangers' eyes turn toward her, look away.

"A sherry, please." She huddles on a bar stool, keeping her back to the Vogue models.

"... it's a Marilyn Brooks. She makes all my clothes..."

"... I'm waiting for my agent to call..."

"... the CBC producer just phoned. I have to drive to Toronto tomorrow..."

"... I'm here to relax. I'm not going to write anything new. Just revise..."

A blonde girl in clothes Molly's daughter Pat would call 'funky,' joins her.

"Hi, I'm Martha Morrison." Dear God. The film critic.

"I'm Molly MacLeod." *Oh. A slip. My own name.*

"McLeod... What do you write?"

"Short fiction."

"Who's your publisher?"

"I don't have one."

"Oh... A scotch," Martha says to the bartender. She takes her drink and swivels around on the stool. "Married?"

"Yes. And you?" Molly asks.

"Sort of. I live with a guy."

"... How come there are so many women? Who organized this, anyway?"

"... Relax. I've a deadline for my novel. The field is yours." This from the Marilyn Brooks client.

"... They're mostly married."

"... Open marriages?"

Martha giggles and nudges Molly, nodding towards the voices.

Molly blurts, "My God, I feel old! A fraud. I haven't published anything since the 60s."

"Where?"

"Literary magazines, quarterlies."

"That's okay. Don't let the big talkers get you down. They're only here for the hunt anyway."

The hunt?

Molly follows Martha to dinner. They are joined by Rod somebody, a playwright. Molly senses the instant chemistry between these two. She's the third that makes the crowd. When she sees all the strange faces, she panics and feels herself floating upwards.

"Excuse me," she says. She pulls out her chair and rushes to her room, opens her typewriter, reels in a sheet of paper. If she starts to write, maybe typing will keep her inside her body. First my name, she thinks. Types 'Molly MacLeod.' Oh. Supposed to be O'Hara. She stares at the paper.

Molly MacLeod. Her old byline. The name in her university annual. She decides to keep it; centres the type. A title? Finds none. This fighting floating is a lot like being drunk. She remembers the first time she ever got drunk, and giggles. It was VE Day. Everyone was celebrating. No one was caring, just pouring. She was only seventeen, underage, and knocking back rye and apple juice. She became wild, obsessed with 'losing my virginity,' and tried to seduce the high school chemistry teacher. It was a small town, but people were kind. The next day they just smiled and said things like, 'Everybody does something crazy once in a while,' and patted her shoulder when she slunk down the street, humiliated and hung-over. She types, *When People Were Kind.*

She hears other typewriters clacking down the hall. Nice, everyone working like that. She struggles. The words seem meaningless, Scrabble words. But in her struggle the scary floaty feeling does go away. She frowns, stuck for a word.

Begins again. Starts and stops; starts and stops; then changes into her nightgown and curls up in bed.

She awakes early, dresses and goes out for a morning run. She finds herself looking around. At the lake. At trees. She slows down to a jog, then a walk, as she reaches the lodge. She showers, puts on a fresh tracksuit, and heads for the dining room.

At breakfast she sits with two French-Canadian women, poets. They are gentle, warm, and too polite to question her about publishers. She focuses on them and avoids the other writers. After breakfast she lies in her room all day and skips lunch, but drags herself to the pool before dinner.

She sits with the lively French-Canadian women again, but talk is difficult. For months the only socializing she'd done was with the Daffodil Ladies—the volunteers at Princess Margaret Hospital. She knows all about chemotherapy and radiation, but hasn't kept up with books, plays. Everybody here has. And she has never gone anywhere on her own—always with Patrick, Phoebe, or the kids. That evening she stays in her room and knits, hears 'the others' dance and drink below.

Alone, she is forced to think. About Phoebe, about herself; forced to realize that her loyalty to Phoebe arose from her own need. The need to feel that surge of relief when she rushed into Phoebe's room and found her still alive.

She feels alienated from the people here because she's published so little. After marrying Patrick she was content with domestic creativity—baking bread, tending flowers in the garden, preserving jams and jellies from their fruit trees, taking trips with him to educational conferences, going places with Brian and Patsy. But mostly, hanging out with Phoebe and Phoebe's artist friends. 'A gallery groupie.'

The next morning there was a new arrival, a friendly Newfoundlander, Peggy Hamilton. A plump, curly-headed woman with rosy cheeks; a woman her own age. She was chatty and Molly liked her immediately. A published author, but modest and unpretentious. After breakfast Peggy dropped into her room to chat and left a copy of her book. Molly told her she was going home a week early.

"I'm just wasting time here, Peggy. I don't think I should stay on..."

"Wait," Peggy advised. "It takes time, starting again. Stare at the typewriter long enough, and you'll write. We've all gone through it, you know?"

Molly doesn't know. She rips her day's writing—her name and address, and a beginning to her teen-age story— from the typewriter, crumples it up and hurls it into the waste basket. *Who cares about my dumb youth?*

She showers, changes into her old flannel nightgown, huddles under the covers.

Another morning. Mornings are awful, because when she wakes up she's still looking down at her body on the bed. She forces herself to look away, outside. The sun is streaming through the curtains. She gets up to drink coffee, to go out for a run. Moving works, brings her down, so she dresses and tiptoes through the silent lodge and jogs out to the highway. Thick white frost covers the ground and glues fallen leaves together. They will thaw, dry out, turn brown, blow away.

Me, too, she decides. I'm going home. She slows down, sighing.

She carries grief like a backpack. Each day a victory. Today, she thinks, I got up, didn't I? Through trees an icy lake shimmers under the sun.

She heads for the coffee maker in the empty dining room. Its light glows in the early morning darkness. She pours a cup, warms her hands around it. A sleepy stranger enters. He looks young, shy, confused. About Andy's age, she guesses.

"Coffee?"

"Please."

She passes the young man cream and sugar, watches him. He is slight, dark, has pared facial bones like Nureyev's. She likes men's bones.

She extends her hand. "My name is Molly... Molly Mac-Leod." Oh. She's done it again. MacLeod.

"I'm Jean-Claude. My English is little."

"Montreal?"

"Trois Rivières."

Feeling motherly puts her at ease. When she hears the breakfast crowd approach she says to the new arrival, "Come on out and meet the others." She leads him to the lobby and introduces him. He puts down his cup and shakes hands. He is very solemn, very formal, until Molly introduces him to Cecile and Marguerite. Then he becomes animated, using his own language. Molly pats his shoulder and leaves, but the three follow her and demand that she sit with them.

Breakfast is the only meal she can manage, but she realizes this new person and his francophone friends will speak English out of politeness to her. She rises. "I'm into a story," she says. "See you later."

He rises, the two women smile.

In her room, she rolls a fresh sheet of paper into the typewriter. Stares. Begins.

She works all morning, is late for lunch. When she arrives she sees Jean-Claude at the far end of the table, already surrounded by female admirers. She smiles, remembers, 'the hunt.' He waves; his smile is bright.

Later, Peggy drops by. "I'm inviting you to a happy hour before dinner. I've asked that new fellow, Jean-Claude, you know?"

"Okay. Oh, you know what? You were right. I tried the-staring-at-the-typewriter trick. It worked."

"Grand. Let me see what you've done, girl. Finish the story first, though."

Alone in her room she is restless and cannot write, is still afraid of floating upwards. She goes to the pool and swims. She thinks, God, I'm fit! Three-mile walks each morning, forty-length swims every afternoon. She climbs out of the pool and bounds upstairs. Dripping and towel-wrapped, she fumbles for her key. Jean-Claude opens his door. All she can focus on are those marvellous eyes, with their changing, amazing colours. Dark brown, almost black, but caught by the light, a golden topaz.

"Hi." Jean-Claude raises a glass. A greeting? Curiosity at so much noise? An invitation?

"Hi." She darts into her room and shuts the door. She showers, washes her hair, snuggles under a quilt and reads Peggy's book. She enjoys the Newfie expressiveness, the old values. It's good to have another friend, she thinks. Not as exciting as Phoebe, of course. More like me. Old. Square.

She walks to the mirror and for the first time in months really sees herself. Dull brown hair, hazel eyes. Blah. A mess. Phoebe was right. Not that she was ever in Phoebe's league, even if she had tried. She takes the new sweater, the scarf and velvet slacks from the drawer and puts them on. She carefully applies lipstick, eyeshadow. When she brushes her hair, she finds a flash of silver starting to grow just off centre. She decides she likes it, and changes the part to show it off. *There. Not bad.*

She had brought a bottle of sherry from town for her room to avoid bar chatter, shyness. She pours a glass, then puts it down. This is silly! Drinking wine so she won't panic, so she won't float upwards just because she's going to visit new people.

If Phoebe were here everything would be lively. Molly used to trail in Phoebe's wake, watching heads turn. Red-headed Phoebe, flamboyant enough to wear pinks, purple. People stared at Phoebe and knew she was somebody; wanted to join them, to make friends. Molly was always popular when with Phoebe, became part of things, made friends.

She gulps down the sherry, strides out towards Peggy's open door.

"I was afraid you wouldn't come, you know?" Peggy says. "I'd have fetched you. You should mix more, if you don't mind my saying so?"

Molly smiles at the way Peggy raises her voice, turning statements into questions. Maybe they are questions.

When Jean-Claude arrives, Peggy waves towards the opened wine. "Help yourself there." He pours a glass and raises it. Molly watches him move, lithe as a dancer. Phoebe would fall for him, she thinks, and have an affair. Phoebe the great lover. Breasts gone, uterus gone. Life gone.

Wine sticks in Molly's throat. Her hand trembles.

Peggy is talking about her husband, her children, her novel. Molly swallows, sips again.

Jean-Claude turns to her, "And you, what do you write?"

"Short stories. Used to. Not lately."

"Ah-h, me too. I like them best. So exciting, so intense, so…" He closes his hand tightly into a fist, trying to explain.

"Compressed?"

"Yes. So fast. In the novel one gets lost."

"Right, with short stories, the end is always in sight."

"Exactly. How long are you here."

"Two weeks."

"Like me."

"No. I have been here already one week. I'm going home next Sunday." *Surprise. I'm staying. What were we really talking about? Why is Peggy smiling?*

Jean-Claude fills their glasses. "I am dizzy," he says, "from all the English."

There are loud voices in the hall of the others going to dinner.

"I have to go back to my room for a minute," Molly says. "I'll see you later." She kisses Peggy's cheek quickly, waves at Jean-Claude as she darts off.

She needs distance, suddenly, and more time to think.

Back in her room she sits on the bed. There are too many feelings, too many people, too many complications. Why? Because she is beginning to enjoy herself and she is making new friends. Scary. She rises and goes down to dinner.

When she reaches the dining room there is only one seat left, two tables away from Peggy and Jean-Claude. She feels sudden warmth. From the wine? She's been cold so long. She smells wonderful smells: broccoli, squash, roast beef, potatoes. She slathers horseradish on the beef, feels it burning her nose. Wonderful! She is embarrassed by her sudden appetite, eats dinner as if starved. She washes down hot apple pie with strong sweet coffee.

She slips away quickly back to her room to work on an Icelandic sweater for Andy. At home, the concentration it required had been an escape, but just now, in ten minutes, she has wrecked several hours work. She flings it on the dresser. Damn Patrick, Beth. And damn Phoebe.

Peggy knocks before opening the door. "Come on down, now, Molly," she calls. "Don't be sitting in here all alone. You're missing the fun. Everybody's dancing down there. Jean-Claude, he said to tell you he'd come up and bring you down himself if I didn't."

"I'll bet." Molly stalls.

Peggy commands, "Hurry, girl."

Molly picks up her knitting and says, "Okay, Peggy. You win. I can at least bring my knitting down and watch the others."

When they reach the lounge, Molly sees Jean-Claude dancing with Martha Morrison in her Annie Hall clothes. It is a slow dance and they are holding each other close, cheek-to-cheek. What happened to Rod, Molly wonders, and plunks down near the bar.

Savagely, she grabs her knitting. The needles are weapons, weapons against the young. She peers over her glasses, thinking, I'm a grandmother. Might as well act the part. When Jean-Claude spots her, he winks. But his cheek is still tight against Martha's. Molly forces a smile and watches the other dancers, all swaying and laughing.

When the music ends she rushes to a lounge chair and pretends to knit. No sooner has she begun to count, or to pretend to count, than the music stops and another record starts. Jean-Claude crosses the floor and stands before her. He touches her arm, reaches out for her knitting, takes it from her and sets it aside. As he lifts her to her feet she thinks, I didn't even struggle.

She is responding to the feel of him. To his hands, his shoulders.

Rod cuts in. "Madame Defarge," he says. "You've finally stopped knitting and watching for the guillotine. You're joining the party." His comment strikes her as terribly funny, and as she stands between him and Jean-Claude she bends over in uncontrollable laughter. She shakes with laughter, so convulsive that she excuses herself, afraid to look back at Rod's bewildered amusement, at Jean-Claude's concern.

Her giggles change to sobs as she runs upstairs and flings herself on the bed. Now she cries for the first time since Phoebe tried to tell her she was dying. Heaving, gasping sobs. *I thought she needed me to be strong, optimistic. That was my own need. I wouldn't listen to her, just rambled on about medical breakthroughs, her stamina. No wonder Phoebe was being very specific about the wig she sent me to buy from Anthony, her hairdresser, who wept. She made me feel her skull and buy that wig to try to make me face it. Poor Phoebe, you knew me well.*

I'm older than Phoebe. Fifty. I will die too. So will Patrick, Brian, Patsy, Beth, Peggy, Jean-Claude. Everybody.

Her tears finally exhausted, Molly sits up on the bed, grabs a Kleenex and dries her eyes. She walks over to the mirror, looks. Fifty.

Was Jean-Claude flirting with me, she wonders. Sex is a good antidote for grief; youth for age. Phoebe had affairs. Why not me? Patrick pushed me here. It would serve him bloody right.

She goes over to the sink, throws cold water on her face, re-applies makeup, heads back downstairs to the lounge, searching for Peggy.

Jean-Claude stands up in surprise, strides across the room to meet her and hand her a cognac. *"Santé!"* he says. "I was worried. If you did not come, I was going to bring you a nightcap."

"Thanks. That was sweet. Something just seemed too funny."

"No. I watch you. Not too funny. You needed to—what do they say here, 'let go.' "

"Right."

He looks concerned and puts his arm around her. They click glasses, sip their drinks. Molly forgets Peggy, and leans close to him, feeling comforted and alive. She lets her hand brush his thigh. He moves closer.

Not yet. Better think about this. She rises, says,

"Thank you. I needed that brandy. And your understanding."

"You are leaving again so soon?" He looks confused.

"Yes. I have to work on my story tomorrow. I want to get up early." *And get away from you as fast as possible.*

In bed she listens, hears voices grow quiet, footsteps pass, doors close. She enjoys the sounds, the lulling hum of voices.

But at sunrise she is still awake. Jean-Claude. He's just a kid. But so warm.

She dresses quickly and jogs down an old logging trail. In the clearing, she sees milkweed, its dry pods bursting, white fluff spilling out, brown seeds clinging. She slows down and reaches for a stem, touches it. The fluff feels like silk in her fingers. Lovely. She lingers, then suddenly straightens up. My story, she remembers. She jogs back, showers and goes to her desk.

She looks over yesterday's pages, and leafs through Peggy's thesaurus. There's a sense of recognition, an old familiar feeling, like writing essays at university. Rushing to make the quarterly deadline. She is writing about the first time she met Phoebe at Banff. Both teen-agers during the war. Sometimes Molly giggles aloud, remembering Phoebe showing her how to pick up guys. Phoebe telling her how to dress, how to put on make-up. Both sharing their dreams. Phoebe's to paint, Molly's to write. Phoebe died, but she realized her dreams. Exhibits in Paris, Rome, New York.

Molly resumes typing. She works all day, skips breakfast and lunch. Late in the afternoon she slides a complete first draft under Peggy's door, then wanders around the lakeshore, savouring afternoon sun that warms her back.

When she returns, she finds a note tacked to her door. From Jean-Claude, inviting her to join him and Peggy for drinks.

She bathes and changes, but does not cross the hall until she hears Peggy's voice there first.

She arrives at his open door and surveys his room. He has possessed it, made it beautiful. Crazy paintings are everywhere; branches spill from bottles. *Another artist.*

"Come in, Molly, we were waiting for you," Peggy says.

Jean-Claude smiles and pours them wine. Then he shows them his sketches. Faces at the table, at the bar. Sharp, wild, intense. Molly pauses before a sketch on his dresser. A woman's face. A crazy, sad face. Jean-Claude watches her, smiles at her curiosity.

"We saw you, Molly, you know?" Peggy says. "Up on the hill there? We were looking for you. Jean-Claude wanted flowers, so he picked those branches. Just weeds, but see how grand they look the way he's fixed them?"

"Did you see the milkweed?" Molly blurts. She has missed two meals and feels the wine hit. She raves on, her hands describing bursting pods. Jean-Claude is curious.

"Milkweed? Many colours? *L'oiseaux du paradis?*"

NO. Birds-of-Paradise... Phoebe's favourite flower. Masses of them at her funeral. Molly breathes deeply, says, "No, not Birds-of-Paradise. No colours. Grey, white, brown." She turns hopefully to Peggy, who shakes her head. "Peggy? Help!"

"I don't know French either."

Jean-Claude offers to fill their glasses.

"No thanks," Peggy says. "But it's good, isn't it Molly?"

"Yes."

"Another?" Jean-Claude offers.

"No thanks."

"Why?"

"I didn't eat much today. I'm already tipsy. I'll talk too much."

He sets the bottle down, his face earnest. "I, too, must be prudent. Prudent?" He looks to them to see if he has used the correct words. The women nod. He continues. "After all, I am getting on. I am thirty-five." Molly suppresses a smile. Thinks gleefully, Andy is only twenty-one. Maybe... They part and agree to meet at dinner.

On her way to the dining room Molly calls on Cecile. "Do you know the French word for 'milkweed?'"

"No, I don't. I should... I have a Larousse, let's look it up." They find nothing. Cecile frowns. "It must be a French-Canadian word," she suggests. "But I've never heard it. Ask Jean-Claude."

"He didn't understand me. I was trying to describe it to him. Never mind."

They chatter during dinner, talk to people across the table. After, Peggy asks, "Are you coming back to the lounge?"

"Yes." She follows them there and picks up a beer. Everyone is dancing. Jean-Claude coaxes, "Come on, Molly."

She moves towards him and they dance, loosely, apart, but keeping eye contact. Soon everybody is singing. Molly smiles. Tonight, she realizes she has made friends with people she had hated on sight. She is having fun. Jean-Claude is like Phoebe, she thinks. He gets me involved, gets me moving.

After everyone straggles off to bed, Molly lies awake. She is listening, wondering if Martha Morrison is across the hall with Jean-Claude.

Next day she sleeps in and awakes stretching happily, eager to get out on the road. She walks along the lake to pick milkweed, choosing carefully. Some have ripe brown pods ready to break; others are bursting, and spill out fluff and seeds; and there is one with pods still green, yet to ripen. Yes, these.

She carries them back to the lodge. Upstairs, she knocks on Jean-Claude's door. When he opens it she announces, "See? This is the plant I was talking about."

He laughs. "How foolish I was! This is my favourite, this crazy plant. And in French it has such a wonderful name. It is called *coton sauvage*. A nice name, yes?"

"Yes." Wonderful, yes, she thinks. Literally 'wild cotton.' Messy, erratic, productive. At its best in autumn.

"Come in, help me arrange these." He takes her hand.

"No, I can't."

"But you must listen. You must learn something wonderful about this plant. Do you know why I love *coton sauvage*? It is beautiful, yes. But I am, like Nabokov, a lover of *les papillons*... butterflies. It is my great hobby... No, my passion."

"But what have butterflies got to do with milkweed?"

"*Coton sauvage* is the food of the Monarch, the great one, the most beautiful, my favourite."

"How exciting!" she says. "The Monarchs are gorgeous. I've gone to Presqu'ile Point in the fall, just to see them. Thousands of them fluttering, a mass of bronze, setting off for Mexico. All those colours! But I still don't get it—the connection—milkweed with butterflies."

"You will understand, let me explain. The pupa or larva, could not become a great beautiful butterfly, without this plant, *coton sauvage*. It is the food, the nourishment from it, that enables the larva to survive, that gives the Monarch wings."

"Wonderful," she says. And is moved, somehow, by this information.

She is very tempted now. Not only is Jean-Claude beautiful, but he has shared this magic knowledge, and she has learned that they both have a passion for the Monarch butterfly.

He beckons her to sit down. He pats the space beside him on his bed, invites her.

Magic, she thinks. Too much. *No.*

She bends down and embraces him. "Thanks for telling me all that. But I'll never get out of my own cocoon if I don't get back to work."

He shrugs. "I understand," he says. "And I forgive you. But you must work. Okay?"

"I will. Save me a place at breakfast?"

"Of course."

He stays in his doorway holding the milkweed, smiling as she strides across the hall.

She showers, changes, gives herself a once-over in the mirror and goes downstairs to join Peggy and Jean-Claude who have saved her a place at their table.

For the rest of the week they become a threesome, sit together at meals, walk together before dinner. She and Jean-Claude swim alone because Peggy is afraid of water. He reaches for her in the pool. She swims away. He laughs, persists, grabs her foot; she kicks, splashes; continues swimming lengths. Tempting. Seriously tempting.

But Molly remembers. 'Gallery groupie,' 'shadow.' Now she understands. No. She goes back to her room and continues writing. Phoebe died, but when alive she always had a future, a present, a past. I became a part of other people's lives, Molly realizes. Phoebe's friend, Patrick's wife, Brian and Patsy's mother. Now I am finally present. I have a future.

HER last morning she makes the rounds. Hugs and kisses; exchange of addresses. She and Peggy cling to each other and promise to write.

Molly knows that she must find Jean-Claude, although she would prefer to avoid their goodbye. She decides to go back to check her room. This is an obsession of hers, when travelling, this fear of leaving something behind. Herself? What self?

Jean-Claude is waiting by her door. "So. You are really going now?"

"Yes."

"Forever?"

"Of course forever..." She stops. It is too hard to explain. We are all going forever, she thinks. and I just got here.

"One minute, please, Molly. Your address. Come." He holds her hand, leads her to his room. He closes the door and tightens his arm around her waist, hands her paper, a pen. "Your address."

She writes and as she does he kisses the back of her neck, pulls her around close to him, kisses her mouth. He is warm, alive, pulling her towards his bed...

So warm, so alive...

No! He is no more her solution than Phoebe, Patrick or the kids had been.

"No," she says. "I will really miss you. I'll write..."

He shrugs, makes a face, then kisses her lightly.

"Send me your stories... Just a minute, Molly. This is for you, I did this one for you." He takes the little painting from the dresser.

"Thank you." She clutches it, and kisses him. "Goodbye," she says and returns to her room.

She puts the little painting in her briefcase and goes for a last walk alone.

* * *

RIDING home on the bus Molly savours the autumn landscape and watches how the trees show more colours further south. Phoebe colours. Orange and red.

She clutches her briefcase. Drafts of three stories. Peggy liked them enough to spend a whole morning writing suggestions in the margins, asking questions. Molly smiled, reading Peggy's scrawls—'Tell me more about this, girl.'

And she'd insisted that Molly send her the revisions, saying, 'I've just got to see what you're going to do next. How these turn out.' The drunken teen-ager one; the one about herself and Phoebe; the one about meeting Patrick at university. Molly feels a surge of energy, and knows she will need it to work hard. She must edit, revise, polish. Over and over again. Rough drafts, but all her own. It's a start, but she is impatient, because although she has reclaimed parts of her life, she has so much to do now, so much catching up.

First she will hang up Phoebe's dress, then she will take Jean-Claude's painting to the picture-framer... that weird guy. Really weird, but maybe he'd make another story? Of course. She smiles, remembering her terror—now thinking, what a find! What a character!

She touches the bouquet of milkweed picked after her farewells and strokes the rough nourishing pods. Grey, ripe brown, and pale promising green. Her own colours. Food for fliers.

tape recorder

In memory of Raymond Carver

HAT are some of the influences on your writing?"
Paris Review interviewers always ask that, she
thought.

"Volleyball. I'm a passionate volleyball player. So much
so that my wife resents it."

"I meant artistic influences."

"Oh, we're talking artistic, are we? Well then, Henry
Moore and Bartok. I spent a whole year listening to Bartok, in
1982, to celebrate his anniversary."

The woman frowned. She remembered that year.
"You've written about your obsessions," she said. "Could
you elaborate?"

"I thought you wanted artistic. Okay then, the cat. That
damned cat decides what time we get up and when we're
supposed to go to bed. Even when I'm supposed to work.
You could sure say the cat is an influence and an obsession.
My wife's obsession. She's crazy about that bloody cat."

The woman cleared her throat. "Chekhov is one of your
favourites. Was he an influence, so to speak?"

"Chekhov is dead, so to speak. So how can he be an
influence?"

"I've read that you admire Chekhov."

"Yeah, he's okay. I suppose you could say I like Chekhov.

But that's sure one dumb question. Writers only talk about themselves. That guy won't want to talk about Chekhov.

"This is my first interview for *Canadian Books* and you're not helping at all, only making things worse. Just answer the goddam questions, dope!"

The man went out to the greenhouse to smoke a cigar. She followed.

"You know I hate cigar smoke. Why are you deliberately harassing me?" He did not answer. He never answered her when he smoked cigars. She went up to the attic for the afternoon and re-read one of the famous author's books.

After a quiet supper of a pizza the woman ordered, her husband said, "Let's practice some more with the tape recorder. That was fun, this morning."

"You've got to be kidding. All I need is more practice with the machine. The right buttons to push, that stuff."

"For sure. You also need practice with the washer and dryer, the toaster, the cuisinart. All that junk down in the basement."

"Shut up. Teach me how to use the tape recorder."

They put the machine on the coffee table. "This button to record," he said. "That to reverse."

"I won't need it to reverse."

"You never know," he said. "That one to stop. The orange one to pause. But for God's sake, don't push record when you want to reverse or you'll lose the whole damn thing."

"I'd never do that."

All week the woman re-read the author's books. Every time she read them she had more questions. She had 33 questions, not counting sub-questions 5b and 5c.

Two days before the interview she typed the questions out. More professional. While she was typing, her husband came home.

"We're on strike."

"Dear God," she said, "just what I need. Of all times!"

He went out to the greenhouse to smoke a cigar. She followed.

"You're supposed to be out on the picket line."

"I'd rather smoke cigars. I've never been on strike. I don't know what to do."

"You might like it. I know the words to *Solidarity Forever*. I'll write them down for you. I've had experience at demonstrations. You'll make new friends."

"I hate that song."

"The media love these strikes. You might be interviewed on TV."

"I want to smoke my cigar."

The wife went up to the attic once again and re-read the author's books.

After a late supper of Kentucky Fried Chicken brought in by her husband, the wife said, "The interview is tomorrow. If we practice the interview again, would you please try to be serious, please?"

"Sure," he said. I like being a famous author. It beats being a community college teacher on strike, married to a wife on strike."

"I'll get paid, you know."

"Sure, I can be serious," he said. "Try me."

The night before her important interview at the Harbourfront International Writers' Festival, her husband got a new battery for the tape recorder. He inserted a new tape. "One, two, three, four, five, testing," he said. The wife watched and listened. She felt professional and secure.

She went up to the attic. She knew she would not sleep but could re-read the author's books. Also sneak out early without waking her husband.

In the morning she did none of her usual morning things. She did not eat hot whole grain cereal with bran on top. She drank lots of coffee.

She did unusual things. She put bath oil in her bath, eye shadow on her eyelids, lipstick on her lips. She looked at herself in the mirror and wiped all the stuff off. She put on an old dress she liked. A bright dress, but comfortable. She was ready to go when her husband came down.

"Thank God," she said. "I thought you'd never get up. What took you so long?"

"I was waiting because I know you like being alone in the morning. You're always mad when I get up."

"Today I need your help. I have to know if it's alright to put the tape recorder in my briefcase. Could anything bad happen to it in there?"

"Not a chance."

"How do I look?"

"Okay."

"One more thing. About those questions, you know? Do you think I should just scrap them?"

"Yeah, wing it. It'll sound more spontaneous."

"That's what I've thought all along."

She put on her old orange poncho and kissed her husband. He's going to make a crack about the poncho, she thought.

"Are you sure I look okay?"

"You look fine."

"And you really think I should scrap all the questions?"

"Yep."

She took a deep breath. "Goodbye."

"Good luck," he said. She dropped her briefcase and moaned.

"Now it'll be awful and it's all your fault. You're supposed to say, 'Break a leg.' "

"I was only trying to be supportive. So go break a leg, then."

"It's too late for that now."

SHE rode on the bus to the fancy hotel. She was afraid of big buildings because she'd grown up in a small town. Not today. She had her briefcase.

She went up to a couple of security guards at an information desk.

"Where is the press hospitality room for the Harbourfront International Writers' Festival?" They looked at her briefcase, at her poncho, at each other. One of them spoke. "There's nothing like that here, nossir."

"But I'm late, it's got to be here! The readings are here!" Shrugs. The woman walked away, down a long slippery hallway. She saw a girl behind another information desk. She went up to her.

"I'm looking for the press hospitality room for the Harbourfront International Writers' Festival," she said. "See, here's the phone number."

"Want me to call?"

"Please." The girl telephoned. "Wrong hotel," she said, pointing. "Down the street."

The woman ran across the marble floor with her briefcase. She tripped and fell. She got up. "Dear God!" she said.

It was raining outside. She ran through the rain to the right hotel. She entered but came out in a parking-lot. Another entrance. I hope no one saw me, she thought.

In the lobby were chesterfields, lamps, people, and an information desk.

"Could you please direct me to the elevator that goes to the press hospitality room for the Harbourfront International Writers' Festival?"

A girl looked at a chart. "Down that way — across to the very end, then up to room 871."

"Thank you." Across the lobby to the elevator, up to the eighth floor. And to room 871. Inside was a table full of different kinds of booze.

A girl came up to her. "Hello," she said.

"I'm the interviewer from *Canadian Books*? I've an interview with the famous author at 11?"

"He's in another interview. Would you like a coffee?"

"No thanks."

The woman looked around, recognized various other famous authors. Golly, she thought. A tall skinny guy in leather gave her and her briefcase a dirty look. He turned to one of the famous authors. "*Canadian Books* isn't worth bothering about," he said. The famous author nodded.

Another girl, an official-looking girl, came in with a big man and led him to her. The woman's own famous author.

The woman reached out and shook his hand. Where in God's name will I interview him? she thought. All those mean guys.

"Would you like some coffee?" this new girl asked.

"No."

"Would you like something?" This to the famous author.

"Coke." He smiled at the woman while the girl got his coke. The woman smiled back. He took the coke, said, "Come this way. My room's right around the corner. It'll be quiet."

"Fine." She darted past, nearly spilling his coke while he held the door.

"Thank God I'm out of there," she said. "Those kind of people make me nervous."

"Me, too," he said.

"But I'm not afraid of you, even though you're a famous author. We're both Westerners and from the working class."

"Well, well," he said. There was a juggling of briefcases, coke, keys. They entered his room.

She took off her poncho, threw it on a chair; pulled another chair up close to a low table. The famous author was leaning back in an easy chair drinking coke. She opened the briefcase, took out her tape recorder and put in on the table's very edge, smack up against his knees.

She pressed the record button and cleared her throat. "What do you think Chekhov would say about your writing?"

"Wow!" said the famous author, but never missed a beat. He went on about Chekhov for some time. Then he leaned over and looked at the tape recorder.

"It's not working," he said. "I think you're supposed to push that little black thing on top."

"Of course," she said. "My husband forgot about that." Damn him! She pushed the little black thing.

She cleared her throat. "What do you think Chekhov would say about your work?"

He went on about Chekhov, paused to swig on his coke. She asked about his obsessions, influences, etc., just as she'd done with her husband. At one point the famous author spoke of artists 'sailing with a special compass.' He stopped, surprised. "Gosh, I'm talking in metaphors!"

A knock. He got up to answer the door. The woman pressed STOP on the tape recorder. I've got it down pat, she thought.

"It's the maid," he said. "She's come to clean. We can move into the next room." The woman picked up poncho, briefcase, the author's coke. He picked up the tape recorder. "I think I better take this."

"Thanks." They went through the problems with keys and all the stuff they were carrying.

Inside, the author put her tape recorder on the table; relaxed in an easy chair. She threw her poncho on a couch, set her briefcase down, put his coke on the coffee table.

"You've a soft voice," she said, and pushed the tape recorder close to him. His coke spilt.

"Oh my God, I'm so sorry!"

With her poncho she mopped up the coke.

"It's okay. Leave it alone," he said.

"My husband hates this poncho anyway."

The famous author waited; lit another cigarette.

They were finally settled. She remembered how the author had told her to push the little black knob. She pushed it. The tape flew back to zero.

"We'll play forward a while. I was just about to ask how you felt about italics," she said.

The famous author drew on his cigarette. "I remember."

The tape whirred. She pushed STOP, then ON. No voices.

"Perhaps if you turned the sound up," he said. She turned the sound up. Nothing. The author picked up the machine. She had turned the sound down. He turned it up.

"There," he said. Nothing.

"Don't you know what to do?" she asked.

"No, I don't know how to work these damned things either."

"I could phone my husband."

"Do that."

She dialled and got the hotel's valet service. "There's something wrong with your phone, too," she said. "It must be this room."

"Dial 9 first."

"Of course." She dialled 9, then her number. He bloody well better be home! she thought.

"Hello, dear. I need some help with the tape recorder. We had to change rooms. I pushed STOP, then the little black thing, then FORWARD, but we're not getting any sound."

"Twiddle those little wheels at the side. Just turn the sound up."

"We did that," she said. She did not add 'dope.'

"Who's 'we'? Is he there?"

"Yes," she said. We were half way through."

"I'll fix it when you come home. If you haven't lost the whole damn thing."

"Thanks," she said. "Thanks a lot." She hung up.

"He says it's okay. He says he can fix it when I get home."

"Well, well." The author fooled around with the tape recorder. Then he set it down.

"Just give it another go," he said. "It'll be fine."

She cleared her throat. She breathed deeply. "What do you think of magic realism?"

"I don't like 'schools' or 'themes' as such, but..."

They continued until he mentioned Chekhov again. Full circle. Is he trying to end the interview? she wondered.

"Well, I shouldn't take up any more of your time. Thank you. But if I've lost your metaphors I'll just die."

"Now listen. If it's lost, make it up. Invent." She turned the machine off and put it in her briefcase. Then she put on her coke-stained poncho. As she was about to leave she slumped against the door. "I'll need a miracle to recreate your metaphors."

"I believe in miracles."

"I'm so glad. So do I." She was holding onto the door knob.

"I hope you'll enjoy the reading tonight," he said.

I can take a hint, she thought, and said, "Goodbye."

All the way home on the streetcar, she prayed.

When she walked in, her husband said, "You look like hell. What happened to your poncho? Now it's ready for the rummage sale. Let me see that machine." She waited. The sound came on. 'What do you think of magic realism?'

"You blew it. You lost the first half."

"But that was the best part! How will I remember all his metaphors?"

"I think I'll go for a walk while you transcribe this," said the husband. "I'll leave you alone with your work."

"Thanks a lot." She turned on the machine; listened from the middle to the end. She smiled, hearing the famous author's voice, 'Now listen. If it's lost, make it up. Invent.'

I can do that. The editor will never know. As she reached out to turn the machine off, she heard, 'What would Chekhov say about your writing?' She listened. 'Wow!' Then, 'I'd like him to say of me that he is precise, he is honest, he appreciates and has concern for ordinary people.' The whole first half! It must have been turned on in her briefcase. She'd started somewhere in the middle. The first time. When they changed rooms they started again at the beginning.

She phoned the nice girl at the Harbourfront International Writers' Festival to thank her for arranging the interview. She asked her to tell the famous author that his voice recorded very well. She phoned the editor and told him the interview was fantastic.

She played her husband the whole thing.

"You're some expert. It was all your fault. You told me nothing could happen to the tape recorder in the briefcase, but it must have got turned on when I dropped it."

"And you never lost a line," he said. "It's a bloody miracle."

He took her out to dinner and kept muttering, "I can't believe it."

Before the reading the woman ran up to the famous author. "They're all there! All your metaphors. My husband says it's a miracle."

"Well, well," the big man said. He shook her hand and smiled. Then he turned away and walked towards the podium, chuckling.

What's so funny? she wondered.

the coronation

T HE boatman hoists the gangplank behind me after I leap aboard. He nods and tips his cap in greeting before he secures the rope.

Clang! I made it. The ferry.

What am I doing here? Why should I be rushing to attend a party on Ward's Island? 'Celebration,' my young friend Iris called it when she invited me. Celebrating what? Whom? Islanders and artists—and Iris is both—are bad with information, stingy with details. It's neither a book-launching nor an art-opening I reason, if it's being held in her cottage. A house-warming, I guess.

My attendance, or rather, the fact that it was assumed I would attend, seemed a *fait accompli*. Now I can't even remember Iris' actual call or her invitation. It's all a blank.

Why am I even bothering to go to this dumb party? Is it vanity? Was I just flattered, at my grey age, at being invited to join this young crowd?

All social events make me edgy, but especially those held on islands. I don't like islands. There's always that feeling of being captive. Miss a boat and you're a prisoner. Devil's Island, Ellis Island.

I head upstairs to the top deck. There I enjoy the brisk breeze and the mist, even though it's a windy grey evening. It's no summer crossing, this, no.

I like Iris, but not her sister Rose. Nor do I like their bratty little sister Lily. Especially, I do not like their crazy mother,

whom I have never even met, for naming her daughters after
flowers. Why did she do that? Was she a frustrated gardener?
Nursery. But she's long gone, their mother. Maybe that's why
Iris likes me. I'm a replacement.

A teen-age couple at the end of my bench are necking.
Their hands grope eagerly under their ponchos. I smile and
leave them to each other.

I walk to the rail and lean over to watch the water, the
boat's wake. There's froth, and sinister dark currents.

Wake. We call pre-funeral gatherings wakes. Is it because
surface gaiety, like froth, hides a sinister pull to darkness? I
turn around and lean my back against the rail, staring across
the deck, away from the water.

There's chatter as a new group ascends to the upper deck.
It's the usual crowd of urban escapees carrying blankets and
six-packs, and Island shoppers toting groceries and kids;
animal lovers bringing dogs to run and spoil the beaches.

I lurch against the rail and grab it to brace myself. Thump!
There's always that crunch with Island landings. Is bad
eyesight compulsory for ferry boat captains, so that they
misjudge distance, space, and land so forcefully? Or is it a
special skill acquired at some ferry captain's school? A crash
course? We lurch, stumble, clutch our belongings. I tighten
my arm around a litre of French red in a brown paper bag.

Well, that's one thing to look forward to and get me
through the celebration. Everybody else serves white these
days. Chilled. So cold. Red wine is comfort, warmth. Blood.
Communion.

I walk carefully down to the lower deck where passengers are crowding against metal lattice gates. They push,
shove, jostle as though their lives depend on it. The boatman
smiles at their desperation. I pause on the iron stairs, because
I know from experience that he will wait as long as possible
to open that gate. I clutch the rail with my free hand, and

marvel that no one has fallen and fractured a skull on the iron staircase during these violent landings. (A long time ago, when my son was about fourteen, he fell against the rail and knocked out a front tooth. After a two thousand dollar orthodontia job.)

Now the passengers begin to funnel out, marching up the gangplank, crossing the dock. Some mount bicycles; others walk towards homes, beaches. Dogs on leashes pull their owners. I follow the crowd and stroll along the Bayfront path towards Iris' weatherbeaten cottage.

Like most Islanders, she is always on the move. Ward's to Algonquin, back to Ward's, Bayfront to Second Street, et cetera. I turn at Second Street and walk to her new house. Number 29.

Bicycles lean against grey insulbrick; there's a strong smell of cat; green hyacinths pierce mud at the side of the wall. The front steps have been removed, awaiting some never-to-be-completed renovation. I walk around to the back.

I hear party sounds: laughter, music, shouts. "Wanta beer?" I reach a side door. This door is pale purple, and on it Iris has painted (cute, cute) a deeper purple iris. I let myself in without knocking, the Island way.

Iris stands before a wooden block table cutting wedges of cheese and putting them on a tray. She turns, smiles, leans towards the living-room door and yells, "She's here!" She smiles, rushes to hug and kiss me, butcher knife waving in the air like a happy sabre-dancer.

"Hi. You look great, Iris." She wears her uniform: plaid shirt and jeans, long brown hair in a single braid. She radiates youth, health, vitality.

I set my bottle of Kressmann's near other bottles beside the cheese and bread trays.

"I'm glad you came," she says, managing a warm hug, although she still brandishes the knife. Iris is always awkward, endearingly clumsy. I chuckle at this—her un- awareness of herself, at the humour of her embracing me while still holding the knife.

"Neat house," I say, circling my arm around her waist. We enter the living room. "Come and meet the others," she says.

Rose holds court in the centre of a roomful of strangers. I know from experience that the drink she gulps is gin-and- tonic. Rose is pretty enough, but she lacks Iris' artistic talent. She compensates for this by making hard-drinking her trademark. She waves one arm at me and winds the other around a slight, dark, curly-haired young man. He grins at me, waves in recognition, and heads across the room.

Who is he? He grabs both my hands tightly in his, kisses my cheek. He thinks he knows me, but I don't remember him.

"I've been waiting for you," he says. He kisses my mouth. A real I-want-you kiss. I respond, then resist. This guy is a mistaken stranger. I pull away. He grabs my hands tighter.

"You don't know me, right? But I know you. You're Elinor. I've been waiting for you..."

Rose interrupts. I'm relieved. She drags a fair older man across the room. "This is his friend." No names. I nod at the newcomer, but can't offer my hand because the dark kid is still holding it. "They live next door. They are our new neighbours." She hiccups, swivels round and leaves these guys with me. The fair man winks, says, "Excuse me," and leaves in pursuit of Rose.

I'm stuck with the dark one, still gazing at me lustfully. It's been a long time since a man looked at me like that. But I'm not flattered because his response to me is inappropriate. The kid has a problem. Some mother thing? He slides an arm around me and grabs my other hand.

"Let's dance."

"No."

"You'll have to, sooner or later. Might as well face it. There's nothing to fear from me, sweetie," he says.

Who says! Not only is he some kind of weirdo, but he's a clinger, and I sense that the more I resist, the more he'll pester me. I decide to go along with him for now, then sneak away early. Some party. Damn Iris. Why me, getting stuck like this?

A fiddler appears and turns off the record-player. He slowly rosins his bow, carefully tucks his fiddle under his chin, and starts to play. Real country music. He's very good, as good a fiddler as my friend Pete. Mr. Fiddleman, we called Pete. Remembering him usually makes me sad, but I'm caught up in the music. My body wants to move, my shoes want to dance. My feet lead me effortlessly through complicated steps which I dance with the dark young man. It's like *The Red Shoes*, that old movie. Yeah. About a ballerina whose shoes run away with her. How come I know these dances? My Ottawa Valley ancestry. The Irish, I guess.

It's difficult, by now, not to be attracted to dark Mr. No-Name because we dance so well together. He holds me close, closer, and he kisses me again. When I realize how much I enjoy this I know it's time to mention the husband and grandchildren.

Before I can decide how to do this, he says, "I know you're married, and I'm crazy about older women."

"You seem to know all about me but I don't know anything about you," I say. "What do you do, for instance?" This conversation. It's like a beginning courtship.

"I'm an undertaker." He smiles. "It's wonderful work. I love it."

I shiver, and try to pull away. He holds me tighter.

He looks at me, amused. "What's wrong? It's really such a beautiful calling, working with the dead. I'm crazy about the dead. Their bodies are so lovely, and their souls…!"

I am suddenly chilled and shiver again. I've allowed myself to be kissed, fondled, and embraced by a crazy stranger who handles corpses. I even enjoyed dancing with him.

Déjà vu. A medical student I know had an anatomy professor who introduced his first year students to cadavers by holding a tea dance in his anatomy lab. "Desensitization," he called it. After the initial shock, the medic told me these dances had been a barrel of fun. Something like that. Yes.

"Actually I've misled you," my partner confesses. He points at the blond guy pursuing Rose. "I'm really only an undertaker's assistant. I work for my friend."

I cringe at his touch and am trying to plan some way to escape, but he fascinates me. Morbidly. I need a drink, I decide. Yes. Red wine. Warm.

"I'll get you some wine. Red, right?" He smiles into my eyes, and slides his hand across my hip as he leaves.

Now I'm frantic. I look for Iris but I can't find her, although I do hear her in the kitchen, talking. I won't follow him. I search for a familiar face among the guests leaning against walls and sprawled on floor cushions. I recognize no one. Okay. I'll focus on this house. Iris has really cleaned the place up. Windows so sparkling I can look right through and see the cottage next door. Home of the undertakers. I turn away. I don't want to look at their house.

The only furniture in the room is all at one end near the front door which doesn't open when I try it. Right beside the door there seems to be some sort of altar on a raised platform. Has Iris or Rose joined some crazy cult? My friend Jessie had a daughter who did that. Became a pagan and swiped Jessie's living-room drapes 'for our altar.'

I'm relieved when I see Iris return bearing a tray of Ritz crackers. I take one, but I do not want to eat it. The dark guy comes back and puts the glass of red wine in my other hand. I giggle. Here I am facing an altar with a wafer in one hand and a glass of wine in the other.

I lift my glass. "Here's to women's ordination." Iris and the guy laugh, we clink glasses and drink.

"By the way, Iris," I ask, "What's with the altar?"

"We got it for the coronation," she answers.

"Cremation," the man says. Now he sounds determined, less charming.

Weird. Jokes aside, I am drawn to this altar, and especially to a large, covered, oval copper dish placed in the centre. This platter—for that's what it looks like—shines orange against the dark wood. I love copper, polished copper, and I am especially drawn to this platter. The way it lights up the grey room. I move closer to inspect it, and see some kind of crest on top. On inspection, the crest appears Celtic like one my grandmother brought from Cork.

"Iris, when did you get this gorgeous platter?"

"We got it for the coronation."

"Cremation!" the dark guy insists.

I touch the cover.

"Don't open it," Iris says. "You mustn't."

The guy moves closer to me, whispers, "Go ahead, look."

I pause and gulp more wine. It warms me, encourages me. So does the kid's arm around my waist. I'm captured now, for sure, so curious about the platter's contents that I trust this morbid stranger instead of my young friend.

There are little handles on either side of the lid. I touch them and turn around to see if Iris is watching. She is.

"I said don't open it, Elinor !"

He nudges me. "Go ahead."

I lift the lid and set it carefully aside on the altar. I'm nervous and excited. The contents must be very important to evoke such strong differing reactions from two people. Is there something wonderful inside? Jewels?

I lean over to look. Ashes. Grey. In a gritty mound. I stare, and see shining through, my own engagement ring.

"My ring, my ring! Iris, where did this stuff come from?"

"From the coronation."

"Cremation! I ought to know," the guy says, "it's my profession."

I want to retrieve my ring and then replace the cover quickly, but I don't want to touch the grisly mess. My hands tremble. What if I knocked the platter over, spilled the ashes? I give up. I carefully cover the platter.

"Oh Elinor, I'm so sorry. I tried to stop you. I didn't want you to know!" Iris wrings her hands.

"Atta girl." The dark youth pats my back.

I break away and run out of the living room, forcing my way through the back door, away from Iris, Rose, strange undertakers, the fiddler. I stumble along the Bayfront path. There's a hazy white light through fog. The last ferry.

I'll make it. I speed up, run faster. I'm breathless.

The boatman watches. The dark man follows.

futures

*T*HE day I was so mad at my husband that I felt like murdering him I went out to the Friendly Futures tea-room to have my fortune told.

I used to consult a fortune-teller there when I worked in Toronto about fifteen years ago. His name was Robert Charles. He was a simpering man, slight and huddled, with something furtive in the way he moved. But over the years his predictions for me actually came true. It must have been the same for his other clients because the Friendly Futures was always crammed full.

I guess he was a sort of underground psychic because no one had written him up yet and he didn't have one of these TV or radio shows where people phone in to ask questions. Word of his abilities spread from office-to-office, from friend-to-friend. But his prices were cheap, so you had to get to the tea-room before noon-hour opening time or you'd wait all afternoon with a roomful of people. Mostly ordinary-looking people: hopeful housewives, sexy secretaries, and greedy guys on their way out east to Greenwood Racetrack. There were also, usually—at least whenever I'd been there—about six or seven atypical people whose clothes, makeup and haircuts set them off as professionals. They seemed sneaky and embarrassed, as if afraid a colleague would pass by and catch them consulting a psychic. The usual crowd—the regulars—enjoyed talking loudly about past revelations come true, but the atypicals didn't talk. I figured they resented giving away secrets that the psychic might use in readings they were paying him for. Thursdays and Saturdays the tea-room was always jammed. Those were lottery days.

I loved the tea-room's name—Friendly Futures—because Robert Charles was in his way, selling futures. Now, having finished my MA program and having learned all about word origins, I liked it even better, because *future* is from the Latin *futuris*, future participle of *esse*, to be. So hopeful, so positive. I hoped he was still at the Friendly Futures, and at his old prices. TV psychics charged $150 for thirty minutes, and even at that price a friend of mine waited six months for an appointment. Robert Charles only charged ten dollars for a tea-cup reading: five dollars extra each for crystal, cards, or tarot.

I consulted him whenever I was depressed or lonely or mad or just needed to hear some good news. Sure enough, in his teacup or his crystal ball Robert Charles always saw a career change (I hated my social work job), and a dark handsome foreigner who would take me travelling to faraway places. Also, he gave me reminders about health. 'Have a check-up,' he'd say, 'just to be on the safe side.' Or, 'a dental problem will be avoided if you keep regular appointments.'

He tossed out these little bits of information like the free samples that rural western door-to-door salesmen used to con my mother. They'd give her can openers or bottle brushes so she'd feel obliged to buy expensive stuff like floor wax and mops.

After Robert Charles' health freebies—which were always timely—I'd say, 'Well, now that I'm here I might as well go for the crystal and cards.' Then for an extra ten bucks, I'd hear the new stuff, the good stuff.

I'd just returned to Toronto after my fellowship ran out to see if my lawyer had arranged for me to collect the monthly income supplement which my husband Ricardo had agreed to a year ago. At that time, even though the separation was at his insistence, Ricardo became sentimental and told me never to worry about money. He'd provide for me if I just left him alone to pursue his second career as a racetrack handicapper.

Ricardo was the predicted dark foreigner. And yes, he had taken me travelling to faraway places. We fought in all the major cities of South America—Rio, Montevideo, Buenos Aires, Santiago, Lima. I got to see those places because at the beginning of our relationship his solution to our quarrels was always geographic. When I first broke up with him in Toronto he left 'forever,' for Brazil. He returned four days later with a job, begging me to marry him. I did. Then our fights and travels started.

We'd fly off somewhere and enjoy a couple of days sightseeing. (There's a colonial house outside Montevideo called Tara exactly like the one in *Gone With the Wind*, built by some millionaire.) Then one of us would say or do something to put the other off. I got up too early for him: he got up too late for me. He wanted to sample local foods or go to the racetrack: I wanted to visit shrines, museums and art galleries.

He thought my early rising made him 'look bad' when I insisted on getting up early and having breakfast alone. (*Cafe con leche; media lunas*—that's *café au lait* and croissants back home in Canada.) Who cared what the hotel staff thought in a foreign country, I argued. Why should I be deprived of the joy of exploring strange cities in the early morning? Street stalls at sunrise, laughter and staccato chatter rising in a crescendo as South America awoke. I refused to wait in bed beside Ricardo who snored loudly, and grunted if I tried to wake him up.

Robert had foreseen my future in the cards. Up to a point. But the more upwardly mobile and outwardly respectable

Ricardo became, the more of a grouch he became. Although since we met he'd moved from a factory assembly line to a tenured job teaching in a community college, this was not enough for him. A millionaire—he had to be a millionaire—and he would achieve this at the racetrack if I would just leave him alone to his computer and his racing form statistics, and a Success Thought Group he joined which involved a lot of positive thinking and a hefty fee from our VISA.

'Ah, yes. The millionaire syndrome,' the marriage counsellor I consulted said, when I told her about Ricardo's obsession with money and his rejection of me. 'We see a lot of this, in immigrants.' When we got nowhere with counselling, I consulted a lawyer. Ricardo was relieved that I was finally agreeing to separate, but not pleased about the lawyer. He found one of his own, recommended by a student on parole. That should have warned me that his slimy lawyer would outsmart mine, Moira Carroll, an Irish feminist, a feminist eager to get to court. Moira was disappointed when I received the fellowship because it prevented a pricey court battle and I wouldn't need support for a year. She warned me that I was letting Ricardo off easy because I never claimed the share of our assets the law entitled me to, and we'd depleted the resources I brought to the marriage during his periods of unemployment while he 'moved up'—mortgages, a pension from my old job, a couple of bonds. When I tried to explain this to Ricardo, he exploded. 'That was your dowry!' When I relayed his comment to Moira, she hit the ceiling. 'What bloody century was he born in! Dowry!' But I let it go. I was too busy packing and cleaning up the house for real estate agents and prospective buyers. I'd have done better financially if we hadn't wasted that year in counselling. By the time I agreed to separate the bottom had fallen out of the real estate market. But we got a decent price and I figured I could afford to live eight years on my half.

In a desperate mood I'd inquired about a fellowship to study linguistics at Michigan State University. I didn't think I had a prayer. When I was actually awarded it my morale really picked up. I could live an extra year, even longer if my degree helped me get a job after graduation. I'd applied to Michigan while housesitting during one of Ricardo's violent periods when his group therapy didn't seem to be working and Moira thought I was in danger. My employer was an old mathematics professor, and I read about an English assistantship vacancy in one of his academic journals. When I wrote to Michigan I mailed my résumé and transcripts in a big manila envelope imprinted with the University of Toronto Department of Mathematics logo. I figured that the ESL department would think I was a mathematics professor, who, late in life had seen the light and was changing careers. That is, when they looked at my birthdate and figured out that I was pushing sixty.

Moira insisted that Ricardo sign an agreement to supplement my income after graduation, which meant I could live as long as I wanted. Ricardo said we wouldn't need any agreement, that I was his best friend, his sweetie-pie, and when he made his millions he'd share it all with me. We did not, he insisted, need a 'piece of paper.'

'Yeah,' Moira retorted. 'I've heard that one before.' But he had signed this agreement, so I was back in Toronto after graduation to collect and to find an affordable apartment. When Ricardo balked after I phoned and asked for a $400 monthly allowance, I phoned Moira. 'We'll have to go to court,' she said. 'You'll need more than a lousy $400, Frances,' she advised. 'That's a third of the budget in the agreement. Ricardo can afford it. He's earning over $50,000 a year.'

'But I'll be getting the Canada Pension,' I said. 'It's enough.'

'It's not. Besides, you can't afford my fee unless you go for more.'

'Forget it!' I blurted, and hung up. The anger I felt towards Ricardo I directed at her. She was safe.

So, here I am, back in Toronto, Frances Murray, MA, needing to see my dentist and my lawyer but giving up on both because I couldn't afford them, heading off to see a psychic. Mad at my lawyer, and especially mad at Ricardo, who had bought an Esplanade condo on the twenty-seventh floor overlooking the bay while I rented a studio in Ann Arbor furnished with the apple crates I'd packed my books in. I wasn't mad about the money. I wear cheap clothes, I should eat less. But Ricardo had signed a legal document, and I had this thing about him laughing at the law. I respect the law. I do not smoke dope, cheat on my income taxes, or smuggle stuff across the border. The law was there to be obeyed. Especially by Ricardo. For fourteen years, he had bragged to me about his 'integrity.' 'I may lose my temper, I may gamble,' he'd say, 'but I've got integrity.' Or, 'Sure, I get fired a lot, but it's because of my integrity.'

I remembered those lines—the integrity lines, but had forgotten some of his others until now. 'Never trust people who keep telling you they're honest. It's a sure sign they're liars,' he'd warned.

In desperation I read Help Wanted ads in *The Globe and Mail*, but there was only one ESL job. In Japan. I was too old to go that far. The worse things looked, the worse I felt. I tried the Cryptic Crosswords because I used to love them and could crack them in about twenty minutes. Now I start analyzing the origins of all the words and can't get past the first clue. Right brain dead; died in Michigan.

On this Toronto trip I was staying out in Parkdale with my friend Becky, a painter, also down on her luck. The recession. People weren't buying abstracts so she was peddling flowery water-colours of irises and trilliums in shop-ping malls to meet her mortgage payments. Becky had no TV or I might have dissipated my anger watching it. Soaps especially. I love soaps because they are so Biblical. The blind see, the lame walk, people come back from the dead. Miracles happen. Soaps renew my faith in ways that are more fun than church.

Liquor might have drowned my anger, but I get hang-overs easily now, and have always tended to telephone long distance when I drink. This urge to communicate was too expensive on my lean budget.

I remembered seeing the Friendly Futures tea-room sign from the King streetcar. I recalled that Robert Charles had seen me through many a crisis. And there were questions I needed answered. Would I get another fellowship? Another fellow?

I slid into my Aquascutum bought at a factory clearance in Ann Arbor. After the break-up I bought quality, but at prices I could afford. Whatever I bought had to last until my death.

I felt better in my classy raincoat which I wore over a dress and stockings. The Friendly Futures is quite a walk from Becky's, so I kicked off my black pumps and put on Reeboks. The shoes looked funny with my sheer dark stock-ings, but what the hell? Who says aging grad students are supposed to look normal? Besides, the outfit might throw Robert Charles off. If he didn't base predictions on my ap-pearance, I'd get the real thing. Those fortune-tellers go a lot by looks.

It was a crisp, golden Canadian autumn day, but I was madder than I can ever remember myself being. Usually when I'm upset, I go for a long, long swim. But I was in Toronto, in October, and a swim in icy Lake Ontario was out of the question.

I arrived at the tea-room early—before noon—to beat the lunch hour crowd. There was a big blonde girl seated at one table, a black guy at another, and two elderly atypicals wearing navy blue dresses and hats. What they all had in common was a look of expectation and excitement. The black guy drummed his fingers on the table and kept smiling to himself. The atypicals leaned across the table whispering and glancing furtively out the window. The blonde twirled her wedding ring and sighed. I stood at the entrance, put on my glasses and read the price chart posted on the wall. Readings, like everything else, had gone up. Now it was $16 for the package, $8 for extras. The aging grey-haired waitress or hostess—or whatever she was—seemed busy in the open kitchen.

Although prices had changed, the decor was exactly the same—still cramped and dark, still with plastic-covered card tables, painted kitchen chairs, dirty-looking sugar bowls, salt-and-pepper shakers. I'd always wondered what those shakers were for, because here they only served stale cookies and tea. I found an empty table, carefully hung my lifetime coat on the back of a paint-chipped chair, and spoke to the plump blonde woman. She wore one of those bulky jumbo hand-knit sweaters so popular in Canada. There were brightly-coloured crossed hockey sticks and a puck worked into the pattern across her ample breast. She could have been playing defence for the Nordiques.

"Does Robert Charles still read here?" I asked.

"Yes," she answered.

"Will he be in today?"

"Yes," she replied, giving her ring another twirl.

"Oh, good," I commented. There were excited murmurs from the tables.

"I always have Diane," the hockey-sweater girl volunteered. "Robert Charles doesn't come in every day. Not any more. You better ask Marge, to make sure, when she's through in the kitchen."

"Thanks," I said. Why not any more? Has he got a phone-in show now? If so, I wouldn't be able to afford him, either.

Marge was in no hurry. I sat down at my table and looked out at the street, an area I knew well when I worked out here in a storefront clinic. Hookers, drunks, and what we used to call 'multi-problem families,' lived around here. People locked into or out of a welfare system. Never a dull moment, but depressing as hell. Fortune-tellers probably gave the residents more hope than professional caregivers did. Today I needed hope. Hope. Old English origin? Old Frisian? Whatever. But hope, yes, Robert Charles had always given me that. I turned my eyes away from the street and watched Marge bustling in the kitchen. She was a harassed-looking woman in a cheap cotton housedress, the kind my mother used to wear. Mother used to tell fortunes. Teacups, cards. People used to phone her long distance if they had a problem, and she'd set up the card-table by the telephone. She never accepted money because she felt her ability was a God-given gift. I remembered that, because in those days—the Depression—we could have used the extra money. Just as I was pondering my mom's ethics, the door opened and a little bell rang. People moved: chairs squeaked. I turned around. Robert Charles was entering.

He seemed taller and more dignified and assertive than I remembered. He had gone grey and had grown a beard. The beard was what must have given him new confidence I thought, because the simpering effect I recalled was gone. But he looked solemn, and much thinner.

"Hello, dear," he said. "How have you been?"

I was thrilled. He actually remembered me, after fifteen years! This man was amazing!

"Good," I answered. He brushed his hand lightly across my shoulder on his way into the kitchen.

Marge brought me tea and stale cookies—those bulk icing-between-layers cookies that are sold in discount grocery stores in poor neighbourhoods. "What'll it be?" she asked.

"Cup and cards." Then I took a deep breath and added, "Tarot." I handed her the money, forking out the extra bucks. She made change from her apron pocket and handed me a soiled worn-out ticket with number 3 printed on it. Why 3? I wondered. I passed on the cookies, gulped down my tea, and concentrated on not thinking about Ricardo. In my experience it seems that psychics are just telepathic, and I didn't want Robert Charles to pick up on my impulse to murder. Go to psychics with a mate, a mortgage, or a horse on your mind and they clue right into it. In the past I never had a tarot reading. I found the symbols scary, not homey and familiar like my mom's old playing cards. But I'd been studying archetypes in an optional literary criticism course, found them fascinating, and read a book of Carl Jung's referring to tarot symbols. In another seminar, in Irish literature, I also learned that Yeats had been heavily into tarot. Tarot could be the real thing, fortune-wise. In my present emergency I needed the best future I could afford. But I would not think about Ricardo. He just made me mad. I suppose, having been dumped, I should have felt depressed.

Depress-ed. I smiled in spite of everything, thinking of that word. In my practice-teaching I'd had to teach a group of South American students.

I began each session with my class by asking, 'How are you today?'

Inevitably each in turn would answer, 'I'm, how they say—depress-ed.' Always sounding out the final syllable.

After I shouted 'Deprest! Deprest!' the homesick Latins would echo the word after me.

We'd start again. I'd ask, 'How are you, class?'

And they'd answer, 'Señora Murray, I am deprest!' All smiling broadly, no longer depress-ed.

I'll concentrate on my daughter, Zoe, I thought, because that morning I had a long conversation with my son-in-law, David, about her. Zoe works for the CBC on heavy-duty, international political things, and was away on assignment in Beirut. I was a nervous wreck during the Gulf War, and so was David. But David is a Scot and holds a lot in. He handles stress well. I freak out.

I finished my tea. There was a pile of soggy leaves in my cup. I knew a lot of leaves were big trouble, major muddle. I turned over the cup so most of the leaves would go into the saucer. Some readers read saucers, too, and I worried about that. But as far as I could remember, Robert Charles was not one of those saucer readers.

He emerged from the kitchen, walked across a short passage and sat down inside a booth. "Are you ready, dear?" he called to me, leaning out.

"Yes." I carried my cup, saucer, and ticket into the booth and sat down. He stared at my dress, which happens to be the nicest thing I own. It's a special print from Nova Scotia, all different colours. A present from Zoe.

"That's a gorgeous dress," he said. "Those patterns remind me of Jacobean tapestries. I like that dress."

"So do I," I said.

He glanced at my ticket which indicated I was going for cup and tarot.

"My, aren't we brave today," he commented. "Tarot. You are growing up." I shrugged.

He was still admiring my dress—it's a very busy pattern—as he swirled out the deck with one hand, making an arc with the cards. Then he smacked them all together tightly.

"Cut," he commanded. I cut.

"Pick nine cards," he said.

I did this quickly. I'm superstitious, I admit it, I believe in all this stuff because I learned it from my mom and Carl Jung. I handed Robert Charles the cards which he divided into three piles. I'd come here because I wanted the goods on Ricardo, wanted my lawyer to get me support, but now I was worrying about Zoe.

Robert Charles picked up my cards and aligned them in some mysterious pattern. He shook his head, then looked directly across at me. He turned a card. "This is the recent past," he explained. "But I can't tell you this," he said, examining the card. He hesitated, "Well, maybe some of it. Let's see... do you know where your daughter is, right now?"

"In big trouble," I said, "if I know her."

"Oh...well if you know that much, I suppose it's all right to proceed. What is wrong with that girl of yours, anyway? Are you aware that she attracts trouble?" He was touching a card with a picture of a young woman holding a sword.

"Not really," I answered. "It's just her job to go where there's trouble."

"Same thing," he said.

I didn't want to argue or get on his wrong side, so I kept quiet.

"She's given you a lot to worry about," he said disapprovingly.

"That's because we're so close."

"Not as close as you and your son, right?"

"That's what she always says," I admitted, then wished I hadn't let that out. My poor little Zoe in Beirut.

"Do you know she doesn't tell you everything? That things are really worse than she lets on?"

Jesus, I thought, and remembered her friend Peggy Nesbitt calling excitedly to tell me she'd had a long distance call from Zoe. From Sri Lanka when the Tamils were acting up. 'I could hear the gunshots right over the phone!' Peggy said. 'Zoe said they were shooting out in front of her hotel.' Zoe just brought me back a *lungi,* as if she'd been on a tour—lots of heavy embroidery on the hem—and taught me how to knot it either above the breast or at the waist over a blouse. The costume was a wild indigo and created a sensation when I wore it to parties, to the pool. When I asked about Sri Lanka all she said was, 'I climbed Mt. Kandy, Mom, in Buddha's steps. Isn't that amazing?' Gunshots. What the hell was happening in Beirut? I wanted to ask, but usually Robert Charles allowed one question, so I decided to save it till the end. After all he was reading my 'past.' Zoe—well her name means life, and although a risk-taker, she always had an instinct that got her through. She'd be okay.

"What's your marital status? I mean right now." Robert held a card that looked like a King. Another sword. I had taken off the rings Ricardo gave me because I planned to sell them. I was wearing an heirloom diamond ring—my mother's, on the third finger, left hand. There was a thin white gap where the wedding-band had been when I was acquiring a tan. I wanted not to believe Robert now, after all of his heavy stuff about Zoe, but I was curious to hear about Ricardo. Towards the end of our counselling sessions, in a joint interview, I learned Ricardo had lied about a lot of things. The Success Thought Group was a cover for a girl named Rosie. They joined this group to give Ricardo an excuse not to come home after work on Thursdays. But he could never keep his mouth shut. Kept talking about 'this little girl.' When the group people phoned to try to get me involved, I considered it. When Ricardo said that he didn't want me to join, I got suspicious and talked to Moira about this 'little girl.'

'Probably more submissive than yourself and with a brand new dowry,' she quipped.

By the time I returned to Toronto, Rosie had dumped Ricardo, but he'd fallen madly in love with a former student. He had never been that romantic, or even that interested in sex, so by now I figured that this new woman had a healthy bank account. (I got this information from a colleague of Ricardo's.) She was an accountant from Hong Kong. Perfect for Ricardo. A business head and money. As smart as Ricardo in the money department. I secretly hoped that just as he'd depleted my assets, she'd deplete his. Take him to the cleaners.

I began to remember a lot of things that went back a few years. A woman with a Chinese accent who had phoned the house at all hours of the night. Ricardo, the sleeper, missed them all, but said it was just a crazy student who had a crush on him.

By then I found a crush on Ricardo hard to believe. He was about forty pounds overweight, never wore the nice shirts or the handwoven ties I had given him, and clung to his flared-bottom pants, even though the waists were tight.

The Success Thought Group and horse racing had been a cover for Rosie, but Rosie had been a cover all along for Beverley, the night-phoner, the alleged crazy student. I'd warned him to be careful about students when he mentioned Beverley's crush. After graduating in electronics she had anglicized her name to Beverley because she lived on Beverley Street.

After one of our counselling sessions—when Ricardo even scared the counsellor by yelling at me and telling me how repulsive I looked, he apologized on the way home.

'It's not your fault,' he'd said. 'It's just that I find all Caucasian women repulsive.' He went on and on rhapsodizing about Beverly, her almond eyes, small bones, tawny flesh. Ricardo had a newly-acquired sensual streak. I was miffed. After fourteen years of marriage, I was the now repulsive Caucasian. Broke. When he kept going on about Asiatic beauty he sounded like a teen-ager who had just discovered sex. He probably had. I'd known and loved other men before Ricardo, and he'd been pretty inept as a lover, as if he didn't have a clue about women. But I'd lived alone for the past six years, was over the hill, and Ricardo was a good conversationalist who played the guitar well. I love the classical guitar.

I did my thesis on the Woods Cree grammar. I hoped to work up north on a reserve after I graduated, so Cree would be practical. It is also a beautiful language. Such an enlightened grammar. No gender, just classification of the world's things as animate or inanimate. But something really important in one's life, say a kettle or a sleigh, could become classified as animate. I wondered what a Cree would make of Ricardo's dumping me. Had I become an inanimate object? But maybe that's how I'd always regarded Ricardo. As an object. Inanimate. Now the guitar...

I felt a touch, heard Robert Charles' voice. "Come back, please, dear. No more dreaming. Answer the question, please. I asked you about your marital status.'"

"Oh...Separated."

"Are you Catholic?"

"Yes."

"Do you go to confession?"

"Not recently. But I probably should." My rage at Ricardo. If adultery in the mind was a sin, what about murderous fantasies? *A stumble off the subway. A fall from his high-priced balcony. A fatal reaction to his flu shot.*

"My dear, you won't need to worry about an annulment." Robert Charles looked startled as he fingered the cards. He stared at me seriously. "Such a reading... I don't know whether I should tell you this, either..."

"Please," I urged. "Go ahead." Hurry! I thought. He was slowing down. Then I really looked at him, saw how tired and drawn he was, how sunken his eyes were.

Despite his new confident carriage and the beard, he looked ill. Cancer? No, no recent chemo—all that hair and beard. AIDS? Yes. I knew the look. A classmate had died from AIDS, and I'd helped care for him. I'd watched all the stages. Now I really observed Robert Charles. What I'd taken to be his improved appearance was a tightening that accentuated his cheek bones. This tightness gave him the tortured expression I'd seen on my friend. Once I made this connection I looked Robert Charles right in the eye with all the love I could project because I knew that he was dying.

He gave me a wan smile and sighed before turning over four cards from a pile on the lower right corner. He raised his eyebrows and sighed again.

"I don't know quite how to put this. As I said, you won't need an annulment, my dear, because you're going to be divorced, Italian style. Do you know what that means?"

I remembered the term, vaguely, from some old movie, but by now it seemed unimportant. I was watching Robert Charles. The poor man.

"Oh... no." I said, now being more convinced about Robert Charles.

"I mean, darling, that someone is going to bump him off." His statement brought me back in a hurry. Ricardo. I came here about Ricardo.

I clutched my head in my hands. " Oh no!"

"Don't worry, dear, it won't be you. You're a beautiful, loving person. You easily become everyone's mother or sister? But he's mixed up with other women. It will be through one of them. One of these women he's mixed up with will cause his death."

"Thank God!" I blurted, thinking, Good for you, Beverley. "I mean, I wouldn't want to do it. I mean, I wouldn't even think of it."

"I know." Robert Charles reached out and patted my hand. "You're a lovely person. He's got bad karma, brought it on himself. Would you say he's a manipulator?"

"Yes."

"So he's asking for it. He's met his match."

If I were still worried about my own future, I suppose this was good news. Not only would Ricardo be out of the picture, that blasted Beverley would end up in jail. But now my future seemed unimportant. I was healthy, alive, ambitious. There was a dying man across the table.

"This is you," he said, and turned over a card in the centre. His face brightened. "The Empress. You're really going to get your act together ... None of the other cards really matter, if you have this." He seemed pleased, even managed a slight smile.

"You don't know where your next meal is coming from," he continued, "but don't worry. You'll be fine. Money is coming. You'll be surprised. And I see you teaching. Do you teach?"

"Not yet."

"You'll teach, maybe do something even more creative..." Just when things were looking good, and he'd got me interested in my own problems again, Robert was slowing down, looking really tired. This was a short fortune as far as his fortunes went, and he hadn't even read my cup. There was only one more card left. Robert Charles turned it over. The Tower. I waited.

He did not invite the usual free question. Instead he

reached out for my hand and grabbed it. Again, I looked into his eyes. They had that dark, frightened look of someone not reconciled to a certain death. Now our roles were reversed, he was looking to me for hope, hope that I knew I could not offer. So I reached across the table, held him tightly in my arms and kissed his cheek. He smiled. A wonderful smile, his first real smile since I'd arrived.

"You've a healing presence," he said. "All the best to you, darling." He kissed my hand, and slumped back in his kitchen chair. When I stood up to leave, he added, "I hope your daughter will be all right, but as far as that husband of yours goes, he's got it coming to him."

I hesitated. "About that Tower card, the one that's beside me? What does it really mean… you know, is it really important?"

"Turmoil, major changes, upheaval."

"Turmoil, eh? Just more of that old stuff. You've seen me through a lot of that."

He smiled. "Yes, love. More of that. But you'll be released, liberated."

"So I'll survive."

"Yes, darling," he said. "You'll survive."

He kept watching me as I opened the door.

"Thanks," I said. He waved.

I stepped out into the sunlight, turned around and looked through the window. Robert Charles was greeting one of the atypicals. She was handing him her ticket as she sat down to wait for her future. From the golden day outside he appeared even more gaunt and pained, bending over the cards, waiting in the shadows.

He had to stay inside facing all those people with their futures. Giving them hope. I walked quickly now. It was such a great day. I would go out and buy groceries, cook up a storm for Becky, go out for a run, to a movie.